CHILDREN OF
BACH

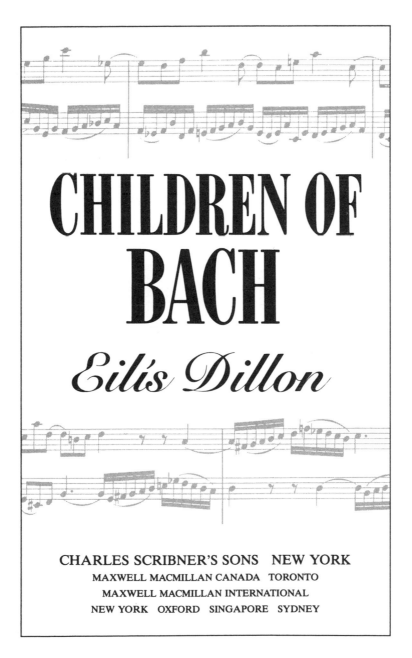

CHILDREN OF BACH

Eilís Dillon

CHARLES SCRIBNER'S SONS   NEW YORK
MAXWELL MACMILLAN CANADA   TORONTO
MAXWELL MACMILLAN INTERNATIONAL
NEW YORK   OXFORD   SINGAPORE   SYDNEY

Charles Scribner's Sons Books for Young Readers
Macmillan Publishing Company
866 Third Avenue, New York, NY 10022

Maxwell Macmillan Canada, Inc.
1200 Eglinton Avenue East, Suite 200
Don Mills, Ontario M3C 3N1

Macmillan Publishing Company is part of
the Maxwell Communication Group of Companies.

First edition   10 9 8 7 6 5 4 3 2 1
Printed in the United States of America

Library of Congress Cataloging-in-Publication Data
Dillon, Eilís, date.
Children of Bach / Eilís Dillon. — 1st ed.
p.   cm.
Summary: A Hungarian Jewish family of talented musicians escapes Nazi persecution during World War II.
ISBN 0-684-19440-6
1. Holocaust, Jewish (1939–1945)—Juvenile fiction.
[1. Holocaust, Jewish (1939–1945)—Fiction.
2. Jews—Hungary—Fiction.
3. World War, 1939–1945—Hungary—Fiction.
4. Musicians—Fiction.
5. Hungary—History—1918–1945—Fiction.]   I. Title.
PZ7.D5792Ch 1992   [Fic]—dc20   91-45432

To the memory of my daughter Máire,
who was a true child of Bach

With so little time for inventory or leavetaking,
You are packing now for the rest of your life
Photographs, medicines, a change of underwear, a book,
A candlestick, a loaf, sardines, needle and thread.
These are your heirlooms, perishables, worldly goods.
What you bring is the same as what you leave behind,
Your last belonging a list of your belongings.

From "Ghetto"—Michael Longley
(In *Gorse Fires*, London: Secker & Warburg, 1991.)

CHILDREN OF
BACH

§ 1 §

Pali was the first to get home, that day. He ran most of the way, his head down, not looking at anyone in case he might see a friend of his parents who had to be spoken to. He had planned this early in the morning, after an argument with Peter. It was Peter who began it by saying, "I'm going to practice in the music room today."

"It's not your turn," Pali said. "You had it two days ago. Suzy had it yesterday and today it's mine."

"You don't need it," Peter said. "You're only nine. You can practice anywhere."

Papa stood up for Pali, saying, "You liked it when you were nine. If it's Pali's turn, he must have it."

Peter had to give in, but still Pali thought it would be better to make sure of his rights. The music room was also the dining room. It was big and cool, with a long, bare parquet floor for walking up and down while you were practicing. In the bedroom you were constantly bumping into the beds or the furniture, and Pali usually finished by standing at the window or even sitting on the bed. Suzy played the cello, so she always had the living room when it was not her turn for the music room. Mama and Papa

1

did their practicing in the morning while the rest of the family was at school.

Little by little, Pali slowed down. Apart from the German soldiers there were very few people about. Those who were on the streets seemed to be walking quickly, too. He went through the square with the fish fountains, then past the butcher's, the vegetable shop, and the huge Wesse Synagogue on Dohóny Street, and at last he turned into Dob Street, his own street.

He felt a little better then, though it was very quiet there, too. The tall apartment buildings seemed blinded by the late March sun, all the windows reflecting gold patches so that you couldn't see through to the rooms. This gave him a feeling of being watched by hundreds of eyes. In the last few days at school he had noticed that some of the other boys were whispering secrets to each other, which stopped when the Jewish boys came close enough to hear. Home always felt better.

He ran all the way up the stairs to the fourth floor. Children were not allowed to use the elevator unless they were with an older person. Peter, who was fourteen, was able to use it because he was tall for his age and was beginning to have dark hairs on his face. Lately he had begun to talk to Pali in a different way, not exactly bullying but somehow taking it for granted that he was better at everything and had special rights. Well, today Papa had settled the argument about practice. Peter's class didn't get out of school so early. Pali would be well established in the music room before Peter could get home.

Pali's hand was on the big brass doorbell before he noticed that the door was standing an inch open. He pushed it gently and slid into the hall. It was very quiet, with an empty, dusty stillness. The door of the living room was open and a shaft of sunlight fell across the hall from the big windows to the front of the house. Then Minna, the cat, walked to the door, stretching her legs fore and aft, obviously having enjoyed a sleep on one of the good chairs. Pali said softly, "Minna! Come here, you wicked cat."

She came running, and rubbed against his ankles saying "Mrrao! Mrrao!" Then she began a gentle purr, as if butter wouldn't melt in her mouth. Pali said, "Sleeping on the cushions, were you? How did you get in? Door open?"

He lifted her up and she hung limply against him until he stroked her head. Then she stiffened suddenly and climbed on his shoulder, pushing her claws through his jersey and kneading his skin with them until he had to drop her. She ran ahead of him into the kitchen.

That door was open, too. Minna went to rub herself against the refrigerator, where she knew the milk was. Pali opened the door and took out the jug, filled her saucer, and watched her for a moment while she concentrated on lapping. The kitchen was rather untidy, the cups and plates from breakfast still in the sink and a cloth partly hanging on the back of a chair, partly lying on the table. Aunt Eva must have gone shopping. If she heard that there was something good in the shops, she would put down everything and hurry to try to get it. Papa always said that Aunt Eva was a great provider, that they would have starved long ago only for her. She was Papa's aunt really. She loved making bread with poppy seeds on top and chocolate in the middle, when she could get those things. She had lived here as long as Pali could remember.

Still, he had an odd feeling that something was different.

Aunt Eva wouldn't have left the kitchen door open, or the living room door. That would be Mama. She was always leaving doors open. Often Papa would come after her and close them, saying in a patient voice, "Laura, the cat. If you want to have a cat you must keep the doors shut."

Mama must be in the music room, or the big bedroom. She sometimes practiced there on a concert day, lying down on the bed from time to time with her violin beside her, doing her relaxing exercises.

There was no one in the music room though the door was closed. So was the door of the big bedroom. Pali opened it cautiously and peeped in. No one. Now he began to run into every room in the apartment: Suzy's room, Aunt Eva's room, and the room he shared with Peter, even the tiny room off the hall where all the coats were hung. The apartment was quite empty.

He went back into the big bedroom and sat on the bed. This was a concert day, though Mama had said the concert might be postponed because of the German soldiers. They had arrived four days ago and were in barracks a few doors away, down the street. It was said that they had come there because they thought it wouldn't be bombed, since it was a residential street. They seemed quiet enough, and Aunt Eva said they didn't speak Hungarian so there was no need to be afraid of them.

Peter said, "I don't see what difference that makes."

"They won't know who is who," Aunt Eva said firmly, with a warning look that told him to be quiet.

Pali got up suddenly and went to open one of the doors of the big wardrobe where his parents kept the things they wore at concerts. There they hung, Papa's black suit with tails and Mama's bright dresses. He reached in and counted the dresses. They were all there, soft silk, all colors. But the bag was gone, the one they packed their clothes in to take to the concert hall. He opened the other door. The bag was not there either.

Then he saw Mama's violin, lying on top of the chest of drawers, with the bow beside it. He rushed back to the kitchen and opened the cupboard door by the sink. The shopping bag was there, the one that Aunt Eva always rolled up and put in her pocket when she went out, because she said you never knew when you might find something to put in it. He tried the closet again, and found that Aunt Eva's fur coat was gone, as well as Mama's. There was no sign of Papa's warm, dark-blue coat, or of his fur hat.

The open front door puzzled him. If they had left in a hurry, they would still have had time to close it. He went back into the big bedroom and picked up Mama's violin. It was clean and polished, as if she hadn't touched it. If she had been practicing, there would have been a faint trace of rosin under the strings. The canvas-covered case of Papa's violin was lying in its usual place under the window where it was in no danger of being kicked. He took it over to the bed and opened the case carefully. The violin was wrapped in the purple silk scarf that Papa had used since he was a student, and that had been given to him by his mother.

Tonight they were supposed to play the Bach Double Concerto together. It was to be here in Budapest, before a huge audience. They shouldn't have gone out at all, on such a day, or if they did, it should only be for a short walk. It was a lovely March day, with the feel of spring about it in spite of the cold. A walk in the park would have been a good thing on such a day. After that they should have practiced a little and then had a rest.

Pali suddenly felt that he might begin to cry. This would make him look ridiculous, when the others came home. Better to keep cool and behave as if he were able to understand everything. He went back into the kitchen and poured himself some milk, then searched the refrigerator for bread. There was a loaf of black bread, rather stale. He cut two slices and sat at the table to eat them, pushing the cloth aside.

The keys of the apartment were there, underneath the cloth. It was Aunt Eva's key ring, the one with the brass owl on it. There were three keys, one for the outer door of the building and one each for the two locks on the front door of the apartment. He sat staring at them for a moment, then picked them up slowly and turned them over and over in his hands.

The whispers he had heard at school sounded louder in his memory. What had they been saying? Jews fenced in, he had heard once, but you don't fence in people. He had begun to tell about it at home but had been told to be quiet. No one seemed to want to listen to anyone these days, least of all to him.

He ate the bread slowly and finished the milk, then went into the music room and took out his violin. He handled it slowly and carefully because his hands felt hot and sticky. There was the cat again. She hated the violin. He put her back into the kitchen and shut the door on her.

As he began to practice, gradually he felt a sort of quietness flow through his whole body. He had learned to drop his shoulders and slacken his arms before beginning, then to pick up the bow and let it dangle for a moment

6

or two, until he was sure that he was not stiff and anxious. Long, slow scales came first, two to a bow, then three, then four, then five, until he reached nine, in a single, continuous movement. Papa had taught him this way of doing it. He often helped him to practice, but Pali's real teacher was a tiny old woman named Mrs. Hilde, who had once taught Papa. Her real name was Mrs. Schafer, but everyone called her Mrs. Hilde. Peter had started with her, too. When you could play Mozart's *Adelaide* Concerto, you moved on to the Franz Liszt Conservatory. That might even be next year, at the rate he was going, but everyone said it was better not to be in too much of a hurry.

He had gone through all of the scales and was working on exercises when he heard the doorbell ring. Here they came, of course. All this worry had been for nothing. But it was only Suzy, swinging her schoolbag, and her friend David who was in Peter's class. She ran past Pali, calling out, "Mama! David is here for lunch and we're going to play together."

"She's not here," Pali said as he closed the door. "No one is here. They've all gone."

David turned green and sat down suddenly on the hall chair. Suzy started clamoring, "Where? Where have they gone? When did they go? Who is gone? When are they coming back?"

"I don't know," Pali said. "I don't know anything. I just came home and found no one here."

"How did you get in?"

"The door was open."

"Thieves," Suzy began, then stopped and went quietly into the kitchen.

Pali and David followed her.

"I saw a crowd, walking," David said after a moment. "They were spread out across the street."

"Who were they?"

"I couldn't see, only their backs, and they were a long way off."

"Aunt Eva, too," Suzy said. "I can't imagine anyone taking her away."

"You think they were taken away?" Pali shouted. "You don't think they just went, themselves?"

"We'll have to wait," Suzy said. "It's no use shouting. Peter will be home soon. He might know something." She pressed her lips together as if to stop herself from adding more, then suddenly said, "I'm hungry. Let's eat something."

There was cold pasta in a bowl in the refrigerator and they heated it with some sauce on the stove. Suzy worked very carefully, so as not to burn the saucepan, turning the pasta over and over with the spoon.

Just as it was ready, the bell rang again.

"Peter," Suzy said. "I'll let him in."

The story had to be told again. They stood in a ring and looked at Peter. Then Suzy said flatly, "You don't look surprised. You know what's happening."

"Yes, I've just heard."

"What have you heard?"

"That everyone was arrested and taken away, the Schlegels and the Waldhorns and the Goldblatts—everyone." He glanced at David and away again. "Your family, too."

"Where were they taken?"

"I don't know. No one knows. Someone said to the brickyard."

8

"To work? To make bricks?"

"No. Just to be locked up there. There's a high wall."

"But they haven't done anything," Pali said furiously.

"You don't have to do anything," Peter said in a new, bitter tone. "It's just being a Jew that counts."

"They were talking at school—" Pali began. He stopped, realizing at last what they had been saying.

"They've been talking for a long time at school," Peter said. "The question is, what will they do next and what should we do in the meantime?"

"You think they'll come for us?" Suzy asked quietly.

"Who knows?" Peter said, and he sounded so like a grown man that they all watched him as if he had the answer to everything. "I know what we'll do next: exactly what we do every day."

"You mean practice? Like on an ordinary day?" Pali asked.

"Yes. If Papa were here he'd say, 'Remember, you're children of Bach. You must play some Bach every single day. That's how to make a musician.' "

"Does it matter if we don't 'make' musicians?" Pali asked after a pause. "Everything will be different now."

"No, it won't. Papa said three days ago that if anything happened we should carry on as usual."

"You mean he knew? He expected this?"

"He seemed to think it would happen. He said lots of people thought it couldn't, in Hungary, but he believed it could happen anywhere."

"Is it happening in other places?"

No one answered Pali, but by the uneasy looks the others exchanged he guessed that this was one of the things they knew because they were older.

9

Peter said, "David, you had better stay with us. There's no point in going home, if everyone is gone."

"I could find out what happened. The neighbors would tell me."

"It might be dangerous."

"But I'm only a boy. They wouldn't want to take me."

"We don't know what they want," Peter said. "You're fourteen. They've taken boys and girls of fourteen. Just stay with us. If we're together, we'll be safer."

§ 2 §

Looking at the trusting faces of the three others, Peter felt heavy and sick, just as he had felt when he had the flu last year. How could he possibly take care of them? Little Pali, with his round brown eyes like a squirrel, and Suzy, tall and willowy but with an innocent face like one of her own dolls, and her friend David, whom Peter hardly knew at all though they were in the same class at school—each one of them seemed to think that he would solve everything and keep them out of danger.

They would have to stay together in order to survive. This was what Papa had said, in that extraordinary conversation they had had three nights ago. It was the day after the German soldiers arrived. Peter had been putting away his schoolbooks and thinking of going to bed when Papa came into the dining room. He sat at the head of the table and began to talk quietly, almost as if he were talking to himself.

"Did you notice a change in people in the last year?" he began, with an anxious look that Peter had never seen on him before. Usually Papa was the one who said one should never worry until after something nasty had happened.

Peter said, "They're quieter. They don't stop to talk as often as they used to do. It's the war, I suppose."

"Yes. It's the war and the general hardship. People have begun to change their habits, even their good habits, and think only of their own safety. They're afraid to trust anyone. There's a different look in their eyes, like animals backed into a corner, fighting for their lives. Some look like foxes, some like wolves. It was only to be expected. People are animals, after all, though they're able to think and plan and write books."

"And play music?" Peter asked.

"Music and painting and books are the only things that lift people above the animals and make them able to feel the presence of God," Papa said. "No matter what comes next, there will always be music."

"What will come?"

"I don't know. I only know what happened in other countries. Being born a Jew became a crime, and the punishment was prison or death. Why shouldn't the same things be done here? My friends say Hungary is too civilized, too cultured, but I don't believe it. Germany was the most civilized country in the world, in its day."

He stood up and walked over to the window, where a few lights showed here and there. Most of them were blacked out, because of the air raids. After a moment he went on, "We should get out, but I think it's too late. You may be able to do it, but I doubt it. They'll block the roads. Some people may help you. You'll know who they

12

are, just by looking at them. Even some of the people you think you can trust will let you down."

"But you and Mama will be here, won't you?" Peter said in a panic.

"Perhaps not. We don't know. If we're not, you'll have to look after the smaller ones."

"You think I'll be able to do it on my own? I couldn't—I'm not old enough."

"That might be a good thing. You have plenty of common sense. Just do what you can. You won't be too frightened?"

"No."

This was the only possible answer. Peter had scarcely seen his father in the days between. He was out most of the time, and when he was at home he looked so preoccupied that Peter was reluctant to take him aside and ask him to explain more about what was going on in the city.

The first two days had been a nightmare, but when nothing happened, Peter began to believe that everything might be the same as it had always been. This afternoon had finished that idea.

Because the others were looking at him, he said in what he hoped was a normal tone, "We must make a few plans. David, tell us about the people you saw walking away."

"It was just when I came out of school. They were so far away that I didn't notice them at first. They were standing all across the street and the traffic lights were red. That must have been what held them up."

"Did you see German soldiers?"

"There were some near me but I couldn't make out if there were any with the crowd. I didn't want to stare too long. Everyone was turning away, almost running, as if they were running from a fire."

"I noticed the people walking very fast, too," Pali said. "You couldn't help feeling that something had happened to frighten them."

"What about you, Suzy? Did you see them?"

"No. I wasn't looking that way, and David said we should hurry."

Then suddenly Pali was crying. They all sat and looked at him, not able to do anything to stop him, until Suzy got up and put her arm around him, saying, "We'll just do what we always do, and wait."

"Wait for what?" Pali said furiously, rubbing the tears away so that his face was streaked with gray. "Wait for them to come and get us, too? Like hens waiting for the fox?"

"That's funny," Peter said. "Papa talked about foxes, and wolves."

"What did he say?"

Pali had stopped crying, which was a good thing.

"He said people are like foxes and wolves," Peter said, "and that we can expect them to behave like that."

"Then they'll lie in wait and spring out on us?" Pali said.

"Not at all," Peter said. "We'll keep a watch for them, and get on with our work. Suzy, after we've eaten, you and David can do the washing up. I'll see if there's any food in the cupboard. Pali, you can look after Minna—"

14

"Why should I do what you tell me? You're not my father!"

Pali was crying again, and shouting at the top of his voice.

Peter said, "Do you want all the neighbors to know what's happening? Keep quiet."

"Now you're shouting, too."

Peter drew a long breath, then said, "You're right. None of us must shout. Is it all right with everyone if I'm the captain of the ship?"

"Yes, yes," they all said, even Pali chiming in at the end.

"Then the first thing is to eat. After that we'll tidy the kitchen and then we'll practice, with mutes."

"Why? I hate playing with a mute."

"So as not to draw attention to the apartment from the street," Peter said patiently. "You won't mind for a while, Pali."

"What about the piano?" David asked. "Suzy and I were going to play sonatas."

"You'll have to use the soft pedal a lot."

They sat around the table and ate the pasta. There was just enough for the four of them, with more black bread and some milk. Peter went rummaging in the cupboard and found enough bread for the evening, as well as a small bag of rice and a carrot.

"It's a very old carrot," he said, holding it up. "I wonder what Aunt Eva was planning for it."

"We'll have to go out sooner or later," David said, "but it might be better to wait until tomorrow. I think I know where to get a cabbage."

15

"Where?"

"In the shop near us, where my grandmother always goes."

"You had better not go too near home," Peter said, and David said, in a thin, dead voice, "I suppose you're right."

After they had washed up and put away the plates and glasses, they separated. Peter went to the dining room. His violin suddenly seemed to weigh a ton and to be all the wrong shape. He had a moment of doubt. Perhaps he shouldn't have said that practice must go on as usual. What if they weren't able to get started? David looked as if he were going to be sick at any moment. He never knew what Suzy was thinking of. Then, from the music room came the sound of Pali playing Ševčík bowing exercises, soft and sweet because of the mute, and a minute later he heard the deep bell-like sound of Suzy tuning her cello while David gently struck the A on the piano.

Peter fitted on his heavy practice mute and tuned his violin, then began on the scale of B-flat in three octaves and thirds. All at once, from the three rooms, the strange, whining mixture of sounds from the different instruments, which he had listened to all his life, seemed to take over his mind. For a few minutes it was actually possible to forget everything else, but that didn't last long. He laid his violin on the table and went to sit down, trying to think back to every word his father had said. It was not very useful. One good thing was that he had said Peter had plenty of common sense. He had never said that before but he seemed to believe it.

From the music room came the sound of Pali playing several top notes out of tune. Peter sprang up, intent on going in there to tell him that it was like a pain in the stomach to listen to him. Then he sat down again with a bump. Pali had stopped for a moment and then had gone back over the exercise again, this time getting it right.

For the first time, Peter began to think about the neighbors in the surrounding apartments. Of course they would hear the sound of practicing, as they always did in the afternoon, though they might possibly know that the children were alone now. Papa hadn't had to wear the yellow star that all the Jews wore, because he was considered so eminent as to be above that kind of treatment, yet someone had managed to have him arrested. Peter began to go over a mental list of the neighbors while he tried to work out which of them would do such a thing. Mrs. Nagy in the apartment next door was always nosy, always noticing what you wore and when you went in and out.

"That's a nice cap," she'd said only last week, looking at it narrowly. "I don't remember seeing that before. When did you get it?"

Peter mumbled that he had had it for a while but hadn't worn it until now.

Another time she'd said, "Your mother always has such nice shoes. I wonder how she manages to get them."

She always seemed to suggest that there had been cheating somewhere, but that was mostly in her tone of voice. She never said so clearly. Whatever the reason, it was very hard to give a polite answer while those beady eyes were on you. And it was hard to avoid running into her. Peter wondered if she was able to hear their front door open and then run to her own, so as to see them going in and out. Whatever the reason, she seemed to be always in her own doorway. He even wondered if she stood there waiting, perhaps with the door open an inch or two. But it was useless to think along those lines. One would end up seeing an enemy behind every door.

The woman in the apartment at the end of the hall was an Italian named Mrs. Rossi. Her husband was there, too, but he was rarely seen except when he was hurrying in or out. He was a professor at the university. Aunt Eva said that Mrs. Rossi had told her he was writing a book. She was quite friendly with Mrs. Rossi but had never been inside the apartment, because Professor Rossi must not be disturbed. Aunt Eva used to meet Mrs. Rossi shopping or waiting for the bus. Now and then she came in for a cup of coffee in the kitchen. She had never complained about the sound of all the practicing. Mrs. Nagy did from time to time. Sometimes she appeared at the door, peering around Aunt Eva's shoulder to see inside, and said in a piteous voice, "I have such a headache today. Would you please ask them to stop early?"

"Certainly," Aunt Eva would say politely. "Don't you think you should take a pill?"

"Yes, thank you, I think I will," she would say faintly, and trail off back to her own apartment.

"Lonely, poor soul," Aunt Eva said tolerantly.

Peter hadn't much sympathy with this, and yet he didn't think that Mrs. Nagy would actually injure anyone. He felt that though she might like to do it, she would draw back at the last moment for one reason or another. For instance, she wouldn't want to go to the police lest they get interested in her, or expect her to keep them supplied with information about everyone. She would be afraid that if she were to be seen with the police, people would find out and hold it against her. The others said of her that she was one of those neighbors who take everything they can get but don't give much in return.

Mrs. Rossi was another story. From what Aunt Eva had said, it seemed that she knew everyone's business and didn't mind being mixed up in it. She gave a sharp look at you, too, but it was a kindly one, not merely inquisitive, and she never tried to pump information out of you. Peter liked her. But now he remembered Papa's words about people being like wolves and foxes. What if Mrs. Rossi were a fox?

There were plenty of other neighbors, of course, and now with the shortage of food some of them might think it would be a good thing to get a few people out of the way, and leave more for everyone else. Peter felt he had given good advice to David, not to go to the food shops near his own house. This meant only one thing, that David should not go home at all. He had probably understood this himself. That could be why he had looked so sick. Peter would have to make up a bed for him on the sofa in the music room, later on.

Peter picked up his violin again and tuned it softly. The others were still practicing. Just as his bow touched the string, the sound of the doorbell seemed to scream through the apartment. At once all the music stopped. Peter put his violin down very slowly, while he fought a feeling of panic. Deep breathing made him a little calmer, just as it did on the stage before a school concert when everyone was watching him. Quietly, he opened the dining-room door and went into the hall.

The two other doors were open and three pairs of eyes

were fixed on him, all blank with fright. He whispered, "Back inside. Keep very quiet."

They did as they were told, without a word. Slowly, he walked to the door, paused for a moment with his hand on the latch, then opened it in one movement.

There on the threshold, so close to the door that it seemed as if she had been listening for sounds from inside, was Mrs. Nagy herself.

3

For a few seconds they stood and gazed at each other. Then Peter stepped aside and said, "Please come in."

She scuttled into the hall and watched as he closed the door. In a half-whisper she said, "Aren't you going to lock it?"

"Why should I?"

"To keep them out. They may come for you, too."

"If they come, the door wouldn't be strong enough to stop them."

She gave him that wolfish look, very direct, with almost expressionless eyes, and said, "You're very brave."

He was glad she was beginning to calm down, since her air of excitement only made everything feel much worse.

"I haven't much choice."

She followed him into the kitchen, looking around curiously as if to see whether they had cleaned it properly. Minna appeared from nowhere and rubbed against her legs, around and around, as if she knew her well. Mrs. Nagy was wearing her usual old brown skirt and jacket, which bagged and sagged all over. Her hair was brown, too, with streaks of gray in it, and wisps trailed down on either side of her face. Peter felt a little sorry for her, she looked so frightened. It was almost as if she were the one who was in danger. He said, "Sit down, please." He pulled out a chair for her and she sat down heavily. "You know what has happened, then."

"Yes. I couldn't miss it. They came pounding up the stairs, marching as if they were on parade, and they knocked at the door—your door. They didn't go to anyone else's. They were very polite. They just said there was a new law, and that everyone in the apartment was to come out."

"You heard them?"

She twisted her hands nervously in her lap, as if she were embarrassed, but the sharpness of her eyes remained the same. Then she said, "Of course I heard them. You couldn't help hearing, with the noise they made. I was afraid they were going to come to all the doors. Why shouldn't they?"

"They're only coming for the Jews."

"How do they know where to find them?"

"I suppose someone tells them."

"That would be a wicked thing to do."

"Yes." He paused, feeling more sorry for her now. Perhaps she did have a heart, after all. More gently, he asked, "Did you see them leave the apartment?"

"That's what I came to tell you. I stood inside my own door, with an inch or so open, and I just peeked out. First your mother came, then your father, then your Aunt Eva. They were very quiet, even your aunt, though she always has so much to say. Two of the soldiers went in front and two behind them, all the way down the stairs. When they had left this floor, I went out on the landing and looked over the banisters. Then I went back and looked out through my own window on to the street. There was quite a crowd there already. I saw them walking away, all together, with the soldiers in front and behind them."

"How many soldiers?"

"Six or seven, including the four who came upstairs. It was hard to count them. They seemed not quite sure what they were supposed to do."

"How did they show that?"

"They didn't keep the same order all the time. Sometimes there were three in front and three at the back, then one or two would move up to the front, to talk to the others, and there would be no one at the back."

"How long did you watch them?"

"Not too long. When they turned the corner, of course I couldn't see them anymore."

"How were they dressed—my parents and Aunt Eva, I mean?"

"Overcoats, just like anyone going out. Your aunt had her fur coat on."

So she really had seen it. Those were the things that were missing from the closet. He couldn't think of any more questions to ask her, and still she sat there, staring at him as if she were waiting for him to say something special. At last she broke the silence by asking, "What will you do now? How will you manage without them?"

"I don't know."

"I won't be able to help you much, but if there is anything I can do, just knock at my door. What about food?"

"There is a little here. I'll have to go out and get some."

"You'll need money. Here."

Suddenly she was rummaging in the pocket of her jacket

23

and handing him a roll of notes. He looked at them in amazement, struck dumb for a moment, before stammering, "Thanks—thank you very much—it's very good of you—I'm sure we'll manage all right—"

"You had better take it," she said. "Food costs more every day. Buy the filling things, like potatoes and pasta, bread if you can get it. The children must have enough to eat. You might find carrots, even chicken."

She stood up quickly and made for the door, then stopped as if she had forgotten something. But Peter saw that she was fixing her eyes sharply on him again.

"Where are the others?" she asked softly.

"They were in their rooms, practicing, until you came in."

"Ah, yes. All of you work so hard. You have talent."

He almost herded her out into the hall. Minna ran after her, as if she wanted her to stay. Mrs. Nagy stooped down and petted the cat, but she had no excuse to delay when he opened the door and held it for her to go outside. Once the door was closed, he leaned his back against it and closed his eyes as if he were trying to shut her out of his mind.

That was impossible, of course. He couldn't make her out. There was something terribly shifty about her, and still the things she said were kindly. It almost seemed, when she was handing him the money, that she was trying to pay him for something. And the way that Minna had behaved, one would think Mrs. Nagy had been in the apartment often and was an old friend. A sort of shiver went through him at the thought that she could be the person who had sent for the soldiers and that now her conscience was troubling her. But if that were the case, surely she would have stayed as far away from them as possible. He hated her question about the others. That seemed almost like a threat.

They were opening their doors cautiously now, looking out at him, for all the world like rabbits peering out of a burrow when the fox is gone. Suzy said after a moment, "She's gone. We heard her coming through the hall and we thought we had better stay out of sight."

"What did she want?" David asked. "Did she just come snooping, or had she something special to say?"

"I can't decide which," Peter said. "She insisted on giving me some money to buy food. I think she meant well."

"Good," Pali said. "I was wondering what we were going to eat when the bread runs out."

"So was I. I only have a little of my pocket money. What about the rest of you?"

They each had some, and they emptied their pockets on to the kitchen table. They all sat around and counted the money. Suzy said, "I'll go shopping after a while, when it gets a little darker. They won't bother with a girl."

"I'll go with you," David said instantly. "You shouldn't go anywhere alone."

"It would be easier to hide if I were alone."

"But if you didn't come back, we wouldn't know where to look for you."

They all stared at each other, shocked at what David had said.

"If you both disappear, we won't know either," Peter said, "but I suppose you're safer together."

This didn't make much sense. After a moment Pali said, "I've been wondering why Mrs. Nagy didn't offer to go and buy food for us herself. It would be easy for her."

"She seemed almost frightened," Peter said. "I thought she was going to tell me something else, and then she just looked at me in a way I didn't like, so I showed her out. Perhaps I should have let her talk."

"I just can't practice anymore," Pali said after a pause. "I can't keep my mind on it. And perhaps it's not such a good thing for people to know we're still here. They'll hear us. Someone might say, 'I thought they had taken away all the Jews, and still there they are.' " His voice was rising as he spoke.

Suzy said quickly, "We've done enough for today, anyway. Let's think of other things now. What about school tomorrow?"

They were all looking at Peter. After all, he had said he was the captain of the ship. He said uneasily, "I don't think we can go to school, at least not for the present. What do the rest of you think?"

"I'd be afraid," Pali said, and the others agreed that they wouldn't be able to concentrate, even if they went.

"Our teacher always skips over me now, when he asks questions," Suzy said. "I think he's hinting that I should stay at home."

"He shouldn't do that," Peter began indignantly, but David said, "He's a nice man. You know him, Peter. He teaches our class sometimes. He doesn't know that I'm a Jew, I suppose, because I'm not dark. You've seen how he avoids asking the Jewish boys and girls questions so that the others won't laugh at them when they fail. If he really thinks it's not safe at school anymore, then we should stay at home."

"I didn't hear him say that."

"No. Of course, he can't say anything. I'm sure he knows much more than we do about what's going on. He says there are no laws against Jews in Hungary, but now it turns out that he's wrong. You don't know what to believe."

"Perhaps he doesn't want us to be afraid," Peter began, then said almost as if he were talking to himself, "There's no point in being afraid until we know what we're afraid of."

The afternoon was growing dark and the blue evening seemed to press in against the window of the kitchen. It looked out on a courtyard, so that you could see across to the other kitchen windows in the apartment house. The lights were going on and people were moving about as they began to cook supper. Then, one by one, the blinds were pulled down. David laughed and said, "They always do that in our house too, so that no one can see what they have to eat. What a life!"

"Let's go, then, and see what we can get," Suzy said.

They divided the money carefully into seven parts, so much for each day of the coming week. David put today's part deep into his trousers pocket, where he could keep his hand on it if he felt anyone coming too close. Then Suzy took the shopping bag and they went out quietly.

There was a deep stillness in the apartment when they had gone. Peter began to think of what Mrs. Nagy had told him, of the little crowd of Jews that she had seen walking off down the street. It made him feel hot with shame, to think of his parents and Aunt Eva being herded like sheep, with barking soldiers yapping around them. So the people in the shop had been right. They had been talking about it when Peter went in to see if they had any chocolate. The shop was on the corner of Dob Street. A man and a woman were telling Mr. Konrád what they had seen. The man kept saying over and over, "To the brickyard, that's where they've taken them, to the brickyard. They're locking them up in the brickyard."

Peter had waited a moment, then had gone quietly out of the shop. None of the three seemed to notice. Mr. Konrád was leaning on the counter with both arms, his face in his hands, while the other two talked. When he had taken a few steps, Peter almost turned back to ask them some questions, but he didn't really need any more information. They hadn't even said who was being taken to the brickyard, but Peter felt that he knew. He didn't know where the brickyard was but there was nothing he could do in any case.

Pali had picked up Minna and was hugging her, so that her purring filled the kitchen.

"Food," Peter said. "What on earth can we give her?"

While he was speaking, the doorbell rang. Pali clutched Minna so suddenly that she squealed and struggled, and finally jumped on to the floor.

"Are you going to answer it?" Pali asked after a moment.

"Of course."

But Peter didn't feel as certain as he sounded. The bell had rung again before he reached the door and opened it a little, expecting he knew not what to be there. It was Mrs. Rossi, standing on the mat, a covered plate in her hand and a wide smile on her face.

"I knew you were alone," she said briskly, "so I thought I'd bring something for your supper."

As he stepped back to let her in, he heard Mrs. Nagy

softly closing her own door. Spying again, of course. Mrs. Rossi must have heard it, too, but she made no comment. She just walked straight into the kitchen and put down her plate, removing the cloth that covered it. A golden cake, like a picture, was sitting there.

"A friend of mine came today with a present of poppy seeds and some flour," she said. "There was too much just for us."

"Thank you."

Peter looked down at the plate, not knowing what to say. It was Pali who asked, "Did you see them go? Mrs. Nagy saw them. The soldiers came to the door and took them away."

"Yes, I saw them," Mrs. Rossi said, and she was not pretending to be cheerful now. "It was dreadful—the worst thing I have ever seen in my life. Your father and mother, artists, the pride of Hungary, taken away like thieves. I thought everyone in the street would run to help them but no one moved. And your aunt, with her shoulders hunched up and her head down, as I've never seen her in all my life."

"No one could have stopped them," Peter said.

"I know. I couldn't do anything myself. I should have rushed at the soldiers and battered them with my fists but I did nothing. We're all to blame."

"Of course you're not to blame," Peter said. "It would be like trying to stop the waves of the sea."

She gave a long sigh, then said, "You're right, of course. But now we have to think and plan what to do next. They're still in the city."

"What can we plan? Do you think we could rescue them? Do you think we could get them home?"

29

"I don't know. I don't even know where they are."

"They're in the brickyard. I heard people talking about it in Mr. Konrád's shop."

"Knowledge is power, they say."

But he knew by her face that this was bad news. On an impulse he asked, "Do you know Mrs. Nagy? She was here a while ago, asking questions. She saw them being taken away."

"I know her, all right," Mrs. Rossi said slowly, "but I don't know much about her. Just don't tell her too much."

"I won't."

"I'll come in again, if I have any news," Mrs. Rossi said. "Knock on my door if you need anything. Be sure to eat up the cake while it's fresh."

"Thank you," Peter said. "It's a beautiful cake."

§ 4 §

When Mrs. Rossi had gone, Pali sat down suddenly at the table and put his head on his arms. Peter shook him by the shoulders and said, "It will be all right. You'll see. We have friends. Everyone wants to help us. We must have courage."

Pali lifted his head and said fiercely, "What's courage, I'd like to know? It would be stupid to have courage now."

"Even if we haven't courage, we must pretend that we have, to ourselves at least. That way we'll get an idea of what to do. And the people who want to help us—no one wants to do anything for a person who whines."

"I'm not whining!"

Peter saw that this was the wrong way. He said, "Mrs. Rossi offered to help."

"She can't do anything. She said so herself."

Peter turned away. He knew that Pali was right, but he was saying things that should never be said. Suddenly he realized that Pali was laughing. Between giggles he said, "Mrs. Nagy looked exactly like the wolf dressed up in Red Riding Hood's grandmother's clothes. I expected her any minute to say, 'The better to eat you with, my dear!' "

a few days. By then you may remember how to make another one."

Peter cut slices for them and more for himself and Pali. As they sat around the table munching, the cake began to look very small. Suzy said, "You can learn, yourself. Plenty of men are able to cook. Look at all the great chefs."

"I wish we had one here now. We could use even a bad chef." All Peter could remember about Aunt Eva making cakes was that there was a bowl of flour and some eggs and sugar on the table. She had never offered to show him what to do with them.

"We could use Aunt Eva," Pali said.

They cooked more pasta but it stuck together and tasted rather nasty without any sauce. Everyone had become very quiet. It was only seven o'clock, much too early to go to bed. They tried turning on the radio but all they could hear was a loud voice barking in German. None of them knew enough German to understand.

"What about cards?" David asked. "Do you know any games?"

"We don't have any cards," Peter said. "Aunt Eva says they only lead to quarrels."

"Dominoes, then?"

They had a set, and they played for a while. The hands of the clock moved so slowly one would think it had stopped. Minna jumped on to Pali's knee and purred loudly, as she only did when she expected one not to move for a long time. Now and then, one of them went into the living room and peered down at the street. Nothing was happening there, though the soldiers could be seen in a little crowd near the house that they were using as a barracks. On one of these trips, by sticking his head right out of the window Peter was able to look a little way down one of the side streets, enough to see it was perfectly empty, too. No news was good news but there was something frightening about the silence.

Back in the kitchen he said, "Nothing whatever is happening. We're quite safe so long as we stay inside."

"How long will we have to stay inside?" That was Pali, of course, beginning to shout again.

"I don't know," Peter said. "We'll have to have patience."

In the next days he used that word over and over again. No one seemed to know what it meant. He hardly knew himself. They couldn't practice all day, and dominoes became a bore after an hour or two. No one seemed to want to read. They went on with schoolwork as far as they could go, but without the teacher it was hard to do anything except read the history and geography books and study some geometry and German grammar. Even Pali, who had always been trying to wriggle out of going to school, said at last, "I think we should try going back. We could just go there and come home again, if we don't like what we see."

"It mightn't be possible to come home," Peter said.

"Why? Couldn't we just say we're leaving?"

"They mightn't let us go."

"They wouldn't be able to stop us."

It was as if he didn't understand at all what was happening around them. The only thing Peter was able to do was to imitate Papa's voice and say firmly, "No. No one is going to school."

He was afraid that Pali would go on objecting, but this

time he didn't. He just went away quietly and sat in the living room with Minna on his knee, and with his head down. It had almost been better when he was putting up a fight. Peter thought of following him but there was nothing he could say.

Mrs. Rossi came each morning with a little news of what was happening in the city. The German soldiers were everywhere and they were still rounding up the Jews. They were able to find them from lists provided by Hungarians who had always hated them and wanted to get rid of them, Mrs. Rossi said. Without those lists, the Germans wouldn't have known where to go.

"They seem to think they have finished with Dob Street," she said. "They're doing the other streets now."

"Then we could go out?"

"They're still in the barracks here, don't forget."

There was no sign of Mrs. Nagy, but he heard her door swish quietly shut each time he let Mrs. Rossi in. Peter didn't like to tell Mrs. Rossi this, for fear of frightening her. If she stopped coming they would have no contact with the outside world at all. She gave him and David lessons in cooking, and she hovered over them while they mixed a cake, saying, "We can't afford to throw anything out. You won't be a real cook until you can throw out your failures. We can't have any failures."

The cake was a bit flat but she said that was because they had no eggs. "Suddenly, all the hens are hiding their eggs, if you're to believe what you hear. I haven't seen an egg for weeks."

But she brought them a whole dozen one morning, saying, "The people who have hens were selling eggs on the street instead of taking them to the shops. Perhaps better

36

times are coming. Now there can be an egg for everyone and some left over for a cake."

Every morning, after Mrs. Rossi had gone away, they practiced scales first, then exercises, then the pieces they were studying, and finally some Bach. David had the living room, because the piano was there, and Suzy used the kitchen, with the pin of the cello held firmly against the leg of the table. This was the best time of the day, when everyone knew exactly what to do and all of them minded their own business. No one was ever allowed to interfere with anyone else's practice. Mrs. Hilde herself had made that rule. She said you could never judge other people's playing better than they could do it themselves. When she was still his teacher Peter had asked once, "What about the critics, then?"

"Critics!" she said, as if he had used a dirty word. "We never think of them."

They had heard no word of her, and she lived too far away to be visited without taking the bus. Pali was the one who talked about her most, since he was still her pupil. Peter could only say that he would try to find out about her, but he guessed that it was no use, that she had probably been taken with all the other Jews to the brickyard.

It was long after dark on the fourth day and they were sitting around the table trying to play a game of dominoes, when there was a short, sharp ring at the bell. It was as if the doorbell had been touched once, very lightly, to make as little noise as possible. Everyone jumped up and stared wildly at the others. No one spoke, afraid of what they would say. When Peter went out of the room, they still stood there, unable to move. He could feel three pairs of eyes boring into his back. Like a sleepwalker, he went

37

to the door and put out his hand to open it. At the last moment he thought wildly, "It's as if the little pigs were opening the door to the wolf."

He opened it a crack and peered out, then burst out laughing. There on the mat was Aunt Eva. She was half stooped, as if she were getting ready to run, but when she saw him she straightened up immediately and darted inside. The others had heard Peter laugh and they all rushed into the hall. For several minutes there was a wild scramble as everyone tried to hug Aunt Eva at the same time, and she tried to hug them all together as well.

David had been hanging back, since he barely knew her from coming now and then to the house. At last she held off the others and looked at him, saying, "I see we have a visitor."

"Yes, we thought he had better stay. He came on the day that—the day that—"

Peter couldn't finish but Aunt Eva said, "Quite right. He's better off here."

"Did you see my family?" David asked very quietly, as if there were no one there but the two of them.

"No, I didn't see them. I had left the group quite early. I don't know if they stopped at your house and gathered in some more. Did you try telephoning?"

"No. Our telephone was cut off a while ago."

"Well, you're safe now," Aunt Eva said. She looked them all over carefully, then said, "All of you look well. You have been taking care of yourselves."

"Yes, and Mrs. Rossi has been in every day," Peter said. "We like her."

"We don't like Mrs. Nagy," Pali said. "She's like the

wolf dressed up as the grandmother in *Little Red Riding Hood*."

"She may be a wolf," Aunt Eva said, "but I'm a lion. Has she come visiting often?"

"Only twice," Peter said. "I don't know what to make of her, really. She says kind things but somehow she looks shifty. She gave us money for food."

"Did she, now? That was certainly a great thing to do, in these hard times. It shows that we must think well of everyone, as long as we can. Most of them are doing what they think is right, God help them."

"Where have you been?" Suzy asked. "We thought you had gone to the brickyard with the others."

"You heard about that? No, I didn't go to the brick-yard." She turned away suddenly, taking off her fur coat as she did so and reaching in to hang it in the closet. "I'd like to sit down and look at you, and tell you what I've been doing since I saw you last."

They all crowded into the kitchen and sat around the table. Suzy put on water to boil for coffee and got out a bowl of sugar and the best cups. Aunt Eva said, "Sugar! You certainly have done well. I'm longing for a cup of coffee."

She waited until she had a cup in front of her, then she gave a long sigh and said, "Well, this is what happened."

39

§ 5 §

"It was not such a great surprise to us," Aunt Eva began. "We had heard that the Jews were being arrested but we weren't quite sure whether or not to believe it. We knew that some people had been moved to another part of the city but since your papa was never obliged to wear a yellow star, we thought we might be safe. Then, after the Germans came, we heard that they were asking about all the people in the different houses, to find out where the Jews were living. That made us very uneasy, I can tell you.

"The day they came, I almost missed them. One minute more and I would have been out of the apartment and in the elevator. I was just on my way to the shops, when I realized that I had forgotten the shopping bag. I had come back to pick it up when I heard them marching on the stairs. One of them—the officer, I suppose—had a list of names. I just said, 'Excuse me,' and started to walk past them, hoping they might think I was the housekeeper, but one of them shouted at me to come back. There was nothing I could do. I was on the list, and when they were sure they had all three of us they made us walk down the stairs in front of them, so there was no chance of escape."

"You left the key behind on the table," Pali said.

"Yes, and I managed to leave the door open a crack."

"How did you do that?"

Aunt Eva laughed. "By holding it open politely and saying, 'After you, gentlemen.' You see, politeness always pays."

"I wouldn't have been polite," Pali said with a snort.

"It was well worth it," Aunt Eva said. "I think that what really saved me was something I found in my pocket. I hate waiting in lines, so I always carry a little book with me, in case I'm held up for a while. I put my hands into my pockets, and there it was in one of them—Voltaire's *Candide*. It's a book about wars, very suitable in fact. I had been in the middle of it.

"As we walked along, I had an idea. I kept very quiet, like everyone else. None of us spoke at all, not even to each other. Then, at the corner of a street a few blocks away from here, the lights changed and we all halted. It was as if we were a line of buses, not people at all. We were spread out across the street. The soldiers didn't know what to do. Some of them seemed to think we should move on, but the others pointed to the red lights and said that meant we should stop."

"I saw that," David said. "Suzy and I were on our way home from school. At least, we saw a crowd stopping like that. I wonder if it was yours."

"It could have been. We were not far from the school. Anyway, there we were, halted, and the soldiers were up at the front of the line, arguing with each other. I just sat down on the curb, and took my little book out of my pocket and began to read. I can tell you I don't want to read Voltaire again for a long time. I was in a sweat, waiting every moment for one of the soldiers to come to the back of the crowd again and yell at me to get up and walk on. I had my answer planned."

"What would you have said?" Peter asked.

"I would have said, 'Sorry, Captain. I was so interested in my book and I wanted to find out what happened next.' Then I would have stood up and gone with the others. But no one came. The lights changed to green and the whole column moved on. Laura—your mama—saw what I was doing but she pretended not to notice. No one else was interested. I suppose they were all too anxious. Anyway, there I was, sitting on the sidewalk, feeling like a fool, still reading my book as if my life depended on it."

"Perhaps it did."

"It looks like that now. The hardest thing was to continue to sit there, without moving, with my nose in my book. It was funny that people just walked around me without taking any notice. I think they had seen what I had done and didn't want to get mixed up in it. I think they just try nowadays to pretend they don't see anything but their own feet."

"How long did you stay sitting on the curb?"

"It felt like five years—it was really more like five minutes, I suppose. I waited until the crowd had turned the corner. It was quite a business trying to see, without showing that I was watching. I kept turning the pages, lifting my head a little each time."

"And were you really reading?" Pali asked. "I wouldn't be able to."

"No, I wasn't reading. I was praying. As soon as I thought it was safe I stood up slowly and walked down the side street, pushing the book into my pocket. I was able to keep my head down while I was doing that, in case anyone I knew was on the street, but I was lucky. I walked for a couple of hours, or what seemed like that, through all kinds of back streets and lanes and alleyways, until I came to my cousin Dóra's house."

Suzy asked, "And you found her there? Wasn't she on a list, too?"

"No. Her father was not a Jew, so she's safe enough. But she nearly died of fright when she saw me. I think she guessed at once that things had taken a turn for the worse. Soon afterward one of her neighbors dropped in, and she had heard that there had been a big roundup. The neighbor is a Jew, too. They were both very frightened but they didn't send me away. Dóra said I should stay inside the house all the time, and that's what I did."

"What about the neighbor? Is she to be trusted?"

"Judit? Dóra said she is," Aunt Eva said doubtfully. "But I was very worried in case I'd brought trouble on them both. That's one reason why I hurried away as soon as I thought it would be safe, and came home. The other reason was to find out how you were getting on." She glanced around the kitchen, then said, "I see you don't need me here at all. You're doing everything so well."

"We do need you, we do, we do!" they all shouted.

Aunt Eva laughed comfortably. "Of course you do. Well, here I am, and we'll soon have everything going on as it always did."

Of course it couldn't be the same, but it felt much better now that she was there. That same evening they had a conference, and she agreed that they had done all the right things. School was out of the question, she said, because there were too many people about and you never knew which of them would betray you. Besides, the situation could change between the time of their leaving home and the closing of school, and they might not be able to get away.

"That's just what I thought," Peter said. "We've been reading."

"And practicing, I hope?"

"Yes, yes, all of us. Bach every day."

"Good. Who has been doing the shopping?"

"We take it in turns. It's Pali's turn next."

"Will you do it now?" Pali asked anxiously. "I don't think you should."

"I think you're right," she said. "The less anyone sees of me now, the better."

"Mrs. Rossi comes often," Suzy reminded her. "Should we try to put her off?"

"I don't think so," Aunt Eva said after a moment. "I think she's a friendly person—at least she has always been friendly to me. She says the Italians have nothing against the Jews, that we're all the same in the sight of God."

"I like her," Pali said, "but Mrs. Nagy is nasty."

"That's not fair," Peter said quickly. "She gave us money and she said she'd help us. But there's something about her that I don't like. Do you know her well?"

"Not really," Aunt Eva said. "She used to speak to me but the last few times we met she sort of scuttled past me. Does she come into the apartment now?"

"No," Peter said, "but often when we open the door she's at hers, listening. It's creepy."

"She always did a bit of that," Aunt Eva said. "It's probably only curiosity. Sometimes when I was alone here,

I used to invite her in for a cup of coffee. She liked Minna. She always asked a lot of questions but she never gave any information about herself."

"Then why did you invite her?"

"Just because she was so nervous, I suppose. I was sorry for her."

"I noticed that Minna seemed to know her," Peter said, "but Mrs. Nagy didn't say she used to come to visit you. I wonder why she's so careful."

"God knows. I think she's harmless."

At last Aunt Eva gave a big yawn, which she couldn't conceal. Then she laughed and said, "It's so good to be home. I'm dead tired—I'm longing for my bed."

She had to hug them again and tell them how well they had managed everything while she was away. Best of all was when everyone was in bed and they could feel her warm presence around them, as if the whole house were breathing differently.

In the morning everyone was up early. Aunt Eva had some money that she had got from her cousin, but she said they should keep that until what they had from Mrs. Nagy was used up. Over breakfast they talked about what Pali would buy when he went out.

"Cabbage," she said, "and meat if you see any. Pasta, too. Dóra had horse meat."

"I hate horse meat," Pali said fiercely. "I won't eat it."

"All the more for us," Aunt Eva said calmly. "It's good food when you're hungry. I'll make a stew of it, if you find an onion or two. Then it won't taste so bad. What time of the day do you go shopping?"

"Very early morning," Peter said, "if we can. It might

be noticed if we went during school hours. People might wonder why we're not at school and start asking questions."

"You've thought of everything."

While Pali was out and the others were at their practice they could hear her moving about, doing the things she always did in the house. Suzy took her cello into the living room and practiced sonatas with David, to leave the kitchen free for Aunt Eva. Soon, delicious smells came from in there, where she was making a stew of carrots and potatoes and onions, and boiling a stock of the vegetable skins. Later, they smelled bread, with the special aroma of poppy seeds that her bread always had. Later still, they heard the vacuum cleaner at work in the big bedroom. It all seemed wonderfully comfortable, and clean and orderly.

When Pali came back with his bag of food, he and Aunt Eva went over the things together. Then she gave him some of the hot bread before he went off to the music room. It seemed an age since he had had the argument with Peter about his turn there. Peter never argued now. Pali could hear him practicing in the bedroom, the Paganini *Theme and Variations*. It sounded very strange, played with the mute, like a mouse playing the violin. Quickly, he took a pencil and a piece of paper from his notebook, and drew a sketch of a tall, thin mouse with the violin under his chin and the bow poised over the strings. It was a good beginning and he chuckled over it all the time he was playing scales and exercises.

Lunch was a splendid meal. There was a vegetable stew with fresh bread and cheese, followed by coffee and cake. They had it in the kitchen for convenience but Aunt Eva said, "This evening we'll eat in the dining room. We mustn't get slovenly."

She sat at the head of the table and watched them eat, just as she had always done. It was such a happy moment that none of them was prepared for the ring at the door. Every fork went down, every eye was turned on Aunt Eva. In the short silence, the bell rang again. She sprang up and in one movement opened the drawer of the kitchen table and pushed her plate, with its knife and fork, inside. She shut the drawer and wiped off the table quickly with a cloth, then said softly, "I'll hide in the big bedroom. You can open the door now."

"That bell!" Suzy whispered. "I hate it. I'll go."

She waited until the bedroom door closed behind Aunt Eva before opening the door. Mrs. Nagy, of course.

"I'm sorry I was so slow," Suzy said. "We were in the middle of lunch."

"Can I come in?"

She had slipped past before Suzy could speak, and was on her way to the kitchen. Peter stood up politely but the others just stared. Mrs. Nagy looked from one of them to the other as if she had never seen them before.

"You're all alone," she said. "I heard the vacuum cleaner. I smelled the cooking. I thought they had come back."

"We've got to keep the place clean," Suzy said. "We've learned how to cook."

Mrs. Nagy looked into the bowl of stew and said, "You certainly have. And fresh bread. It's as good as your Aunt Eva's bread." Then she actually sat down in Aunt Eva's place at the head of the table and said, "Please go on eating. Don't let me interrupt you."

"Would you like some?" Suzy asked in despair. If she began to eat, there was no knowing when she would go away. "Let me give you some stew."

"No, thank you. I've just had some, at home."

But she didn't move, all the same. It seemed rude to go on eating but the others followed Peter's lead and picked up their forks. There was an embarrassed silence. Suzy's chair was in front of the drawer, so she could be sure that it wouldn't be opened by mistake. It was not hard to see that Mrs. Nagy suspected a mystery. She was clearly puzzled by the things she had observed. No one could think of anything to say. It looked as if she would sit there forever, or until she had found out what was going on.

Then, suddenly, while they watched in amazement, she began to cry. Big tears rolled down her faded cheeks, and she seemed to shake all over with terrible sobs while she fumbled in her pocket for a handkerchief. Suzy sprang up and went to put her arm around the old woman's shoulders, saying, "Please, Mrs. Nagy! What's the matter? Oh, do tell us, what can we do for you?"

It was difficult to make out her answer, because her face was all muffled in her handkerchief. They could scarcely believe what they heard. She said it again, this time more clearly.

"You can hide me here. That's what you can do. I know—I've heard—they're going to come for me."

"But why?" David asked. "Why should they bother with you? They're only taking the Jews."

She stopped crying as suddenly as she had begun, wiped her face with her handkerchief, and said quite briskly, "That has changed. There's a new law since last week.

They're beginning now to take the people whose parents or grandparents were Jews. My grandmother was Jewish. Any day now they'll come for me. If they find my apartment empty, they'll think I've gone away."

And she looked around, from one of them to the other, with her old sharp-eyed, wolfish expression.

6

Not one of the children was able to say a word. Have Mrs. Nagy in the apartment! It was unthinkable. For days—it seemed like weeks—they had been determined to keep her out, and now suddenly here she was saying that she wanted to move in to stay. And Aunt Eva—what were they to do about her? No one had imagined a disaster of this size.

It was David who spoke first, saying gently, "We are all sorry for you. It's just that every one of us feels like running away but there's no place to go. I think we'll do better to stay in our own houses."

"You heard what I said," she snapped at him. "They've searched here once. They won't come again. If they come to my place and find it empty, they'll think I've gone away." Her eyes narrowed. "I know you. You're not in your own house, so you're not the one to talk. You came now and then on a visit. Now you think you own this house and the people in it. You don't want me to be safe. You only want to save your own skin."

"That's not true!" Suzy said sharply. "We invited him to stay because he has no one at home now."

50

"Of course you would defend him," Mrs. Nagy said. "And what's the difference between inviting him and inviting me, I'd like to know?"

"Let's not argue," Peter said quickly. "Of course we'll do what we can for you, Mrs. Nagy. It's just that we don't feel you would be any safer here than you would be in your own apartment."

"That's for me to decide." She settled herself more comfortably in Aunt Eva's chair. "You need someone in the house to tell you what to do. You're only a crowd of children. You couldn't possibly manage all by yourselves."

A voice at the door said calmly, "They won't have to manage by themselves. I'll take care of them."

Aunt Eva stood there, smiling. Mrs. Nagy's face was a mixture of terror and curiosity, very funny to watch. Then she began to look embarrassed, and at last she mumbled, in a completely different tone from the contemptuous one of a moment ago, "I'm glad to see you back. I didn't know you were here. I just came in to see that the children are all right, that they were able to manage without you."

"They're doing very well, thank you, but I'm glad I came back all the same."

"Did they just let you go?"

"No. I had to work that myself. But I'm here now and there seems to be no need to worry for the moment, unless someone else goes and tells the soldiers."

"No one would do that," Mrs. Nagy said hurriedly. "I'm sure no one would be so wicked."

"I heard you saying that you're getting anxious about your own safety."

"Yes. When I was down at the fortune-teller's I heard it. Everyone was saying there is a new law—"

51

"The fortune-teller! What took you there?"

"Everyone goes, to find out what's going to happen," Mrs. Nagy said rather defiantly. "And you pick up a lot of news there."

Aunt Eva said grimly, "If the news you pick up is as reliable as what you hear from the fortune-teller, I wouldn't set much store by it. Did you think there was any truth in it?"

"How can you tell? I heard one woman saying that her father-in-law was taken because his mother was a Jew. She was in a terrible state. If they've started going back into the older generations, no one is safe. I didn't stay long. I felt I just wanted to get away as soon as possible, so I came in here—"

"To see if the children were getting on all right," Aunt Eva said. "I see. Well, we'll have to think about what is best to be done."

Suddenly Mrs. Nagy was crying again, saying over and over, her voice rising with every phrase, "Please don't give me away—please don't send me home—please take me in—"

Aunt Eva went across to her quickly and slapped her face, hard. "Stop that at once," she said. "Calm down."

"You hit me!" Mrs. Nagy said in a whisper, putting her hand up to her face.

"Of course I did," Aunt Eva said. "I'm sorry it was necessary. It's a well-known cure for hysterics. Now, keep still while we think this out."

Mrs. Nagy sat quietly and stared at her. Peter guessed that Aunt Eva was as uncertain as the rest of them, that she was playing for time while she tried to think out what to do about this new complication. If it was true that Mrs.

Nagy had a Jewish grandmother, it seemed unlikely now that she was the person who had informed on the family. However, she might have done it if she thought it would take suspicion off herself. There was something very odd in her behavior, something that made it difficult to believe anything she said. But there was no mistaking that attack of hysterics they had just seen. No one could have faked it as well as that, not even a professional actor.

Peter glanced at the others and saw that they were just as uncertain as he was. They would hate it if Aunt Eva decided to keep Mrs. Nagy here with them, but how could she withstand such an appeal? Apart from the fact that it would be heartless to turn her out, they would have made an enemy at a time when no one could afford such a thing.

Sure enough, after a minute or two Aunt Eva said, "Well, it looks as if we're all in this together. That woman in the fortune-teller's—did she give any details of what happened to her father-in-law?"

"Just the same as what happened to you, I think," Mrs. Nagy said. "One day he was quietly at home, reading the newspaper, and they knocked on the door and said he was to come with them. He hasn't been seen since."

"What about his family?"

"His wife is dead. His son—the woman's husband—was out at the time, so he escaped."

"They didn't wait for him to come home?"

"No. That's why I think that if they don't find me at home when they come, they just won't come back."

"I wouldn't like to bank on that," Aunt Eva said. "Well, you had better go home and collect a few things for the night."

"Oh, thank you, thank you. You're so good, you were always so good to everyone."

She scuttled out of the kitchen and they heard the door close behind her.

Aunt Eva calmly pulled out the drawer of the table and took out the cold remains of her meal, saying, "I'd better get this inside me before she comes back."

"Do we have to have her back?" Pali asked miserably. "Couldn't we just lock the door and leave her outside?"

"Of course we can't."

"Everything was so nice without her. She'll be all over the place, giving us orders. She said we needed someone to tell us what to do."

"I'll see to her, Pali," Aunt Eva said. "Don't worry about that. If she annoys you, come and stand by me and she won't go on with it. Don't forget, I'm a lion."

Mrs. Nagy seemed to think so, too, when she came back. She was carrying a very small bag, which she put down carefully in a corner of the kitchen. Then she turned around and glared at the children, one after the other, as if she were about to warn them not to touch it. But then a glance at Aunt Eva changed her mind.

Aunt Eva fixed her eyes on her for a moment, as if she were reading her thoughts, then said, "You may as well clear the table and wash the dishes."

Mrs. Nagy almost ran to obey. When they had a conference later in the afternoon, to discuss what they should do next, she sat quietly and said very little. She gazed at Aunt Eva with adoration, as if she expected her to solve all their problems, but she offered no suggestions herself as to what they should do.

"What I don't like," Aunt Eva said, "is the idea of sitting here and waiting for them to come and get us. If we had cleared out two years ago, when we first thought of it, we'd have no troubles now."

"Did you really know about all this two years ago?" Peter asked.

"I can't say we knew about it but we wondered if something of the kind might happen. Still, people don't want to leave their homes and their friends just because they think something nasty might happen. You have to be sure."

"We're sure now, all right," Suzy said. "But isn't it too late to think of going anywhere? Where would we go?"

"I have uncles and aunts in New York," David said. "They asked my father a long time ago to go out there to them, but he said he was a Hungarian and he would never leave his homeland."

"Was that his only reason?" Suzy asked.

"I don't know. He loves our place in the country, where we keep our dogs and horses, and he said New York is all concrete and noise. I only heard him talk about it once."

"We'll need help," Aunt Eva said. "We can't just go out on the street and flag a taxi, or go to the travel agent and book a passage to New York. Now, has anyone an idea?"

"Mrs. Rossi," Suzy said after a moment. "She's always friendly."

"We don't want to get her into trouble," Aunt Eva said quickly.

"No, but she has been coming in and out all the time as if she doesn't care about that."

"Run out now, Suzy, and see if she's at home. If she is, ask her to come in for a cup of coffee," Aunt Eva said. "I'm sorry I can't do it."

"She'll see you. She'll know you're here," Mrs. Nagy said in a hoarse whisper. "Don't you think it's dangerous to let her come in?"

"No more dangerous than letting you in, dear," Aunt Eva said. "Off you go, Suzy."

Mrs. Nagy subsided again, looking like a sick old mouse. Pali began to wish he had a piece of paper and a pencil handy.

Aunt Eva made a pot of coffee and set out cups. In a few minutes, they heard Suzy coming back, and then Mrs. Rossi came flying into the kitchen and wrapped her arms around Aunt Eva, laughing and crying at the same time.

"You're safe, my old friend, you're safe. I thought I would never see you again. And you have been here for days and didn't tell me." She stopped suddenly, then went on more quietly, "But we can't celebrate. Your nephew— and his wonderful wife—our great Hungarian musicians—we shouldn't laugh—we have nothing to laugh about. At least you are here. And our neighbor, Mrs. Nagy. Suzy told me you had come, too."

"She shouldn't have told—" Mrs. Nagy began, but Mrs. Rossi interrupted heartily, "Of course she should. I was going to see you anyway, unless you want to go and hide. Cheer up, old neighbor. We're all in this together."

"You're not in it," Mrs. Nagy muttered, but then she became silent and contented herself with glaring at everyone in turn.

A mouse that wished she was a rat, Pali thought before

turning away from her and attending to what the others were saying.

"We were just saying that we need help," Aunt Eva said as she poured the coffee. "Mrs. Nagy says that things are getting worse. They're counting grandparents now. They may even come back to make a second sweep, or they might come for the children. Not that I think they will," she added quickly, glancing anxiously at Pali, "but you never know what new ideas they may have. And we don't know what help they might get from our neighbors. There are always jealousies."

"Indeed there are." Mrs. Rossi sipped her coffee. "I hear plenty of tales from my own country, but I also hear good things. They have a great many ways there of concealing people who are wanted by the Germans. In Italy we don't always tell the truth and there are times when this sin is very useful."

"What are these ways?"

"False ceilings in houses, rooms that are built so as not to be easily found—in a back garden or in an attic or a storeroom. There are a great many hiding places, and a great many Jews are hidden. Lots of them are in monasteries and convents, disguised as monks and nuns. The pope and the bishops help a lot. But all those things are in Italy. I don't know anything about how things are done here. Perhaps the Hungarians are too honest to undertake such tricks." She gave a teasing look at Mrs. Nagy, obviously trying to make her smile, but it was no use.

After a moment Aunt Eva asked, "Do you think we could be hidden here in Budapest, in a monastery or in a concealed room? Is that what you're suggesting?"

"I'm afraid I wouldn't know how to find such a place, though I wouldn't have much trouble in my own country. It's always like that. When you change countries, there are thousands of things you never find out."

"I wonder if we would be as safe here as anywhere else, after all," Aunt Eva said doubtfully. "If we just stay very quiet and if I never go out, perhaps people will think the children are managing by themselves."

"That mightn't work if food gets scarcer. I've heard that the Germans count the loaves of bread that go into a house and then work out how many people are in there eating them. Of course, you could make sure to manage with what four children would eat, but that might not be enough to keep the soldiers away. Someone might tell. Hungry people do terrible things that they would never do in normal times."

"Then perhaps we should try to get out of the city," Aunt Eva said.

"They have roadblocks to prevent people from leaving. And it's worse when you get outside, from what I hear. Farming people know every single thing that happens, everyone that comes and goes. But I do think we should try to get you out of the country."

"How? If we can't even leave the city, how could we leave the country?"

"There are ways—"

"You just said you don't know anything about this country," Mrs. Nagy interrupted hysterically, then stopped in fright as Aunt Eva gave her a hard look.

"Make up your mind, Mrs. Nagy," Mrs. Rossi said. "I'll include you in the arrangements if you promise not to interfere. I've been thinking about all of you for a long time and I may be able to do something for you, but only if you're not going to cause trouble."

She and Aunt Eva both gazed at Mrs. Nagy for a long moment, as if she were a wasp that had got into the kitchen. Then Mrs. Rossi said briskly, "Well, then, let's get down to plans."

§7§

They all leaned forward eagerly to listen, as if Mrs. Rossi had the whole solution to their problems. Aunt Eva said, "Arrangements are what we need. I must say that I've run out of ideas. What are you thinking of?"

"I hardly know myself, yet," Mrs. Rossi said. "I know of people who have managed to get away, even in these terrible times. I've helped some of them myself. It's a long, dangerous business, whichever method we choose. We would have to trust people we don't know. That's the part I don't like."

"I don't want to do anything dangerous," Mrs. Nagy said with a whimper.

"You came in here because you're already in danger," Mrs. Rossi pointed out. "It seems to me that you have nothing to lose." She went on more kindly, "There are risks in living at any time. Any one of us could be run over by the bus on our way to the shops, even at the best of times. The moment we're born, we begin to take risks."

But it was no use. Mrs. Nagy just looked as if Mrs. Rossi had threatened her with certain death; and though she was very quiet from then onward, she kept twisting her hands together and glancing fearfully at Aunt Eva and then at Mrs. Rossi, as if they were her enemies instead of her friends.

"My father was a teacher in a small town to the east of Milan," Mrs. Rossi said after a moment. "I was brought up in the city but I have a great many cousins and relatives of all kinds in the mountains to the northeast. The war is on in Italy, too, of course, but not everywhere. There are valleys in the mountains where no one has heard a single shot fired, and where the people live in complete peace. They grow their own food and make their own bread. They always did, though I hear there's a shortage of flour now. In ordinary times, the only thing they have to buy is salt. They would only go to the town for clothes and sometimes for pieces of furniture, if they couldn't make them at home."

"What about the Germans?"

"The Germans are everywhere but there are some places where they only pass through, on their way to the Austrian border. There are some Italian fascists left, I've heard, but everyone knows them. You can disagree with them without risking your life. Most of the dangerous kind were from distant places, and they have either left or been killed in the last few months. If I could manage to get you to any one of three places I know in those mountains, you would be safe."

"How does one reach this heaven?" Aunt Eva asked. "We would walk—we would do anything."

"Some have walked but it took many weeks through the mountains, over the Brenner Pass and down the eastern side. A great many have gone by the smaller passes but in some ways that's more dangerous than taking the main roads. In bad weather there can be landslides, and you can have snow even in late spring. You have to walk by night and sleep by day, which makes it harder."

"I was joking," Aunt Eva said in amazement. "Does this really happen?"

"When people are desperate they get extra strength, or else they find out that they have more strength than they knew. Yes, especially in the early days, people walked. There were friendly houses where they could stay by day, or even for a few days if someone in the party was sick. In spite of the rough going, it was always easier in the mountains than in the flat country. The woodcutters and the foresters have huts in remote places where no one goes but themselves. But those walkers were mostly very small groups, a couple of men or boys, never any women. I doubt if the children would be fit for such hardship."

"How did they manage to cross the flat country?"

"There are several methods. I'm not going to tell you until I've arranged one of them for you. The less you know, the better. You'll have to trust me. You, too, Mrs. Nagy. You'll have to promise not to speak of these things to anyone."

"Of course, of course," Mrs. Nagy said hurriedly. "I'll do whatever you say. I'm not going to speak to anyone. I don't speak to anyone at all, these days. Thank you, thank you, for helping us."

Everyone turned to look at her in astonishment. This was the first time she had shown any sign of gratitude. Watching him, Peter saw that Pali was on the brink of saying something, but then he stopped. Poor little Pali— it seemed all wrong for him to have to learn tact. When he picked up Minna and began to pet her, Peter knew he would be silent.

"Now, I'll tell you about my cousins," Mrs. Rossi said. "There are four families, all with houses within a few miles of each other in the mountains. They know everyone in the area because as well as being farmers they're wood-cutters and charcoal burners. Everyone needs wood and charcoal. So they go to all the houses in their district and they know what people think about the important things. It's not like the city. When the charcoal burner drives up with his horse, he has to come into the house, and sit down and drink a glass of wine, and chat for half an hour and tell the news. He hears plenty of news, too, you may be sure."

"What are your cousins' names?" Aunt Eva asked. "It's not a bit too soon to get to know them."

"There's Peppino and Carlo and Nello and Serafino, and their wives, Maria and Franca and Giulia and Angelina. They all have grown-up sons and daughters, so it's quite a big family. You'll be perfectly safe with them, if we can get you there. I know them well from spending summers with them when I was young. We're all much the same age. We had great times then, before all these terrible things began to happen. After I married, my husband and I used to come home from Budapest for a few weeks every summer, and he forgot his Dante and walked in the mountains and became healthy again. That was long ago."

"Those times will come again," Aunt Eva said.

"Please God. Now, you must carry on just as you have been doing, as if nothing had changed. I'll go at once and see about my plans. Sometimes it can take a while to get them under way."

When she had gone, they looked at each other gloomily and Suzy said, "How can we carry on as if nothing had changed?"

"There is plenty to do, between homework and practice," Aunt Eva said. "I'll move into the big bedroom, Mrs. Nagy, and you can have my room. Come along now, and we'll make up the beds."

Mrs. Nagy picked up her little bag and followed her out of the kitchen.

"What do you suppose she has in it?" Pali whispered as soon as she was gone.

"Money, perhaps," Peter said. "It's none of our business. Let's just be very careful to show no interest in it."

Throughout the evening, when anyone went out of the room where they were all sitting, whether it was the kitchen or the living room, Mrs. Nagy followed them with her eyes as far as the door and clearly had difficulty in stopping herself from warning them to keep away from her room. It was so obvious that one almost had to laugh, though there was something nasty in it as well. But as Peter had said, it was none of their business.

In the following days everyone was on edge. Suzy was making a dress for her favorite doll out of a piece of silk that Aunt Eva had given her. The dining room table was covered with scraps of cloth and pins, so that there was no room for Peter's books.

"You ought to have outgrown dolls by now," he said contemptuously. "Dolls are for babies."

She was furious, and began to yell for Aunt Eva. It turned out that Peter was wrong, of course, and he had to apologize. When it was his turn to do the shopping, he went out of the house with a great sense of relief, as if he had never before breathed clean, fresh air. The worst was that he envied Suzy being able to play with her doll while he could do nothing but think of their plight. It seemed that they would never get away, that they would be cooped up forever with Mrs. Nagy.

The thought of those mountains was with him constantly. At night he dreamed of them, of high snowy peaks and deep green valleys where no one ever came except the birds and the wild boars and deer. There were little black bears there, too, Aunt Eva said, and wild goats and foxes, and hares in plenty. It seemed to him that it really was a dream, that no such place could exist, that surely there would be hatred and killing and pain there, too, as there seemed to be everywhere now.

"It's true that those things are everywhere," Aunt Eva said when he talked to her about it, "but there must always be more good than evil in the world. Otherwise we couldn't believe in God."

"Do we believe in God?"

"Of course. He doesn't seem to be doing much for us at the moment, but he'll come back as soon as we let him."

"You think these things are our own fault, then?"

"To some extent. We need a Moses now, to lead us out of the land of our captivity. Perhaps that will be Mrs. Rossi."

She came every evening, and each time they looked at her eagerly, expecting her to have good news for them. In the shops, the customers talked about food and fuel and shoes, and sometimes about the new sweeps that were

65

taking place and the new categories of people who were being arrested. There was no news at all from the captives in the brickyard, and no one dared to go there and find out what was happening. Then they began to hear of the trains that were leaving the city late every night.

It was Peter who first heard talk of them. By now the people in the grocery shop knew him, and it seemed to him that they were talking for his benefit. They didn't look at him or speak to him directly, but one after another they made remarks that he thought were intended for him to hear.

"This is terrible news—they have taken the Jews away. No one knows where they have gone."

"To Germany, or Russia perhaps. But in big closed wagons like cattle—it's not decent—it's sinful."

"It's terrible, indeed. These are Hungarians. They're citizens of Hungary."

"Yes, for many, many years. No one has a right to arrest them just because of their religion."

"They are good citizens. They have never harmed anyone."

"It shouldn't be allowed."

But no one said how it could be stopped. When Peter came home and told what he had heard, David said flatly, "We knew something like this would happen. I've never had any hope for them."

No one was able to answer, not even Aunt Eva, though she did say later in the day that they would have to wait for confirmation of the news. It came with Mrs. Rossi that same evening. One look at her told them that she had bad news.

"But I have good news, too," she said, looking around at the anxious faces. "What have you heard?"

"Peter heard about the trains," David said. "We think they have taken them away, out of the country, perhaps to Germany. Is it true?"

"Yes," she said reluctantly. "I've met people who saw them."

"When?"

"At night. No one is allowed into the station when those trains are going, or so I have heard. I haven't been there myself. Oh, my poor friends, what can I say to you? I never thought such a thing could happen in this country."

"We don't blame this country," Aunt Eva said. "We don't know who is to blame, if anyone is. We only know we have good friends like you, to keep our hearts up."

"Talking of friends, where is Mrs. Nagy?" Mrs. Rossi asked.

"In her own apartment, I think. She goes in there for a while every day."

"I'm glad she has the courage to do that, at least."

"She seems a little more relaxed," Aunt Eva said. "She was really getting me down, with her whining and complaining, though to give her her due she doesn't do it all the time and she always does what I tell her. I hope she'll be able to keep it up. What is your good news?"

"Transport," Mrs. Rossi said. "I'm not sure yet when it will be but I have been told that it will happen."

"What kind of transport?"

"A furniture van. The driver has a permit to drive into Italy with officers' furniture."

"Is he a Hungarian?"

"Yes. He has been in the business all his life, and his father before him. It's a good, reliable firm."

"For furniture, but how about people?"

"He has been doing that, too, but he doesn't know it."

"You mean that the people go in the van, and he drives off and doesn't know they're there?"

"That's what I've been told. It sounds crazy but it has happened several times already."

"How many people each time?"

"You've hit the nail on the head, Eva. Until now, he has never had more than one or two passengers."

"And now he'll have six."

"Unless you divide, unless some of you go by other means."

"I don't want that," Aunt Eva said, looking around at them as if she were counting them. "What would I do if the other means didn't arrive? We should be in this together."

"I would do the same." There was a pause, and then Mrs. Rossi went on, "I'm trying to imagine how it would be, with all of you in the van, where we would put you. You would have to be very quiet. You'd have to live like mice in a cupboard."

"Mice squeak and nibble," Pali said.

"True. But not when the cat is around."

"Minna! What about her?"

"She'll have to stay with me, until you come back."

"You think we'll come back? I don't want to come back, ever," Pali said fiercely.

"You can decide that later," Aunt Eva said calmly. "You might come back to see Minna."

"Or to see me," Mrs. Rossi said. "The trouble is that we don't know when you'll be able to go. We won't get much notice. You'll have to get ready and just come at once, whenever I tell you."

"I hope it will be soon," Aunt Eva said. "The sooner the better."

§ 8 §

During the next days Pali drew dozens of pictures of mice.
They were all sizes and shapes. Some were done only with
lines, some were carefully shaded in, some looked cheerful
and some frightened. He had some of them peering out
of boxes or bags, looking around to see if they were being
watched, some with wicked grins on their faces, some
seeming to snarl viciously at an invisible enemy. He used
pencil for most of them but the fat ones needed charcoal.

He was showing them to Aunt Eva one morning in the
kitchen when Mrs. Nagy appeared at the door. She
stopped when she saw that they were laughing at something, and looked offended. Then she came over to the
table. She picked up one of the drawings, without so much
as asking leave, and said in horror, "Rats! The child is
drawing rats! He's out of his mind!"

Her mouth was open and her hands in the air and her
eyebrows had almost gone up into her hair, so that Pali
itched to do a drawing of a terrified mouse backed into a
corner. All he said was, "They're not rats. They're mice."

"It's exactly the same, there's no difference!"

She almost looked as if she would climb on the table to get away from the very idea of rats.

"Excuse me," Pali said. "It's not the same. Mice are smaller, they have a nicer character, they're quite harmless."

"Harmless! If I saw one here I'd stamp on him, I'd crush him—"

"Much better to call Minna," Aunt Eva said. "Anyway, there are no mice in the apartment, as you must know by now."

Pali was putting away his drawings, half sorry that she had seen them and still glad to know that they had made her so furious. She wouldn't have been, if the drawings were no good. And Aunt Eva had liked them. Later, she said to him quietly, "We must make sure to bring along plenty of drawing paper and pencils for the journey. Some of the time is sure to be very tedious. You might find things to draw while we're on our way."

They began to plan what they would take with them.

"The trouble is that we don't know how much room we'll have for anything except clothes," Aunt Eva reminded them that evening at supper. "We must remember that we're lucky to get out with our skins, and not try to take along things that don't matter, things that can be replaced." She was looking hard at Mrs. Nagy while she said this, and Pali noticed that after a moment Mrs. Nagy dropped her eyes and began to twist her hands in her lap, as she always did when she was angry. "In any case, I'm sure we'll get our instructions from Mrs. Rossi. Whatever she says, we must follow exactly."

"I don't see why," Mrs. Nagy said. "It's all very well

for her. She's staying here quite safely while we go off into all kinds of dangers. She's not God. She can't tell us what to do."

"In this case she's the nearest we can get to God," Aunt Eva said patiently. "Now, I don't want to hear any more about that. We must all make sure that we have a change of clothes, at the very least. I'm sure we'll be allowed to have that much."

"I should hope so," Mrs. Nagy muttered, but she didn't go any further into the question of what she would take.

Soon afterward she went back to her own apartment and Peter said in despair, "Do we really have to take her with us? Couldn't we just slip away at night and leave her here to get on with it?"

"Peter! I'm ashamed of you," Aunt Eva said. "You know very well we can do no such thing. We've undertaken to have her with us and we can't get out of it just because we don't like her."

"She grouses all the time. Her manners are so bad."

"Well, let's not imitate her in that. I'll calm her down after a while."

It was true that in the next few days Mrs. Nagy became much quieter and didn't jump into every conversation and criticize everyone, as she used to do. She spent a lot of time in her own apartment, only coming in for meals or when she thought she heard someone on the stairs. This happened several times a day, but it was much better than having her sitting in the kitchen or the living room all the time, making remarks about everything that was said or done.

Mrs. Rossi agreed that a change of clothes was essential,

but she said it must be understood that even these might have to be abandoned in an emergency.

"What kind of emergency?" Pali asked at once.

"If you were on the point of being discovered and had to run for your lives, you might not think it worth while to stop and pick up things to carry with you—but I'm sure it won't happen like that. So far, everyone who has gone in this van has arrived safely."

"Can I take my violin, then?" Peter asked.

"Yes, a violin is a small thing."

"Can Aunt Eva carry Papa's violin, and Mama's?"

"One, perhaps. Two would be too much for one person."

"I can take the second one," David said. "I certainly won't be able to take the piano."

"What about the cello?" But Suzy knew already that this would be too much to hope for.

"A cello is as big as a person," Mrs. Rossi said. "But you can give it to me to mind for you, until the war is over."

"God knows when that will be," Aunt Eva said, "but the cello will wait for you. My father played that cello of yours, Suzy, and it lay idle for forty years until you needed it. You played it for two years before it began to sound as it used to do for him, and now it's as good as you would find anywhere."

"My goodness, what a long life!" Mrs. Rossi said. "It belonged to your great-grandfather. I must take great care of it for you."

"If I don't have the cello, then can I have one of my dolls?"

"Yes, of course."

"And I can have my bear," Pali said.

"Yes, yes. A bear is small."

Two evenings later Mrs. Rossi came running in, looking very agitated. She sat down deliberately at the table and clasped her hands together. Mrs. Nagy said loudly, "Something has happened. I know it. Look at her. Why is she so excited?"

Mrs. Rossi laughed nervously, then said, "My husband wants both of us to come in and have supper with you this evening. Can I tell him to come?"

"Of course," Aunt Eva said. "It's an honor."

Mrs. Rossi went out to fetch him, while Aunt Eva set two more places at the table.

"We have beans," she said. "This is a good evening for him to come."

"Getting so excited about a husband!" Mrs. Nagy said contemptuously. "Who does she think he is?"

The children had often seen him in the hall or in the elevator, a tall, handsome man with white hair that grew in all directions. He always greeted them politely and held the door for them with a bow, as if they were important ladies and gentlemen. He never asked questions as some of the other neighbors did. There was never any need to squirm and sidle away from him.

"I'm glad he's coming," Peter said. "I was wondering if he approved of what Mrs. Rossi is doing for us."

"She would be sure to have talked to him about all that," Aunt Eva said. "Besides, no one can afford to have a traitor in the house."

And she fixed her eyes on Mrs. Nagy until the muttering

stopped. It was well worth while, because Mrs. Nagy didn't mutter at all while Professor Rossi was in the apartment. Indeed, she watched him with a sort of awed respect all through supper, as if he and not his wife were the one who was doing her a favor. He spoke to her very courteously, as he did to all of them, and said he hoped she would enjoy Italy when she got there.

"I wish I were there now," he said, "but I have no choice. I must stay here and take care of my students. Perhaps I'll see you in Italy next summer."

It was quite late in the evening, and the older people were having a glass of brandy out of the bottle that Professor Rossi had brought with him, when Mrs. Rossi said abruptly, "Four o'clock in the morning, you must be ready. I'll come for you myself."

Without warning, Mrs. Nagy burst into tears and began to say over and over, "I knew there was something going on. I knew there was a trick in it. That's why you came to have supper with us—"

She stopped as suddenly as she had begun and stared at Professor Rossi, looking like a terrified hen. He said calmly, "My dear lady, no wonder you're upset. You do want to go with this good family, don't you? My wife has told me that you decided on that some time ago."

"Yes, yes, of course I want to go, but I'm frightened all the same."

"It won't be for long," he said, still very calmly. "You only have to endure it for a few days, and think of how much depends on it."

"Yes," she whispered. "It's just that I'm frightened."

She was silent then, but her outburst had upset them

all. Peter glanced at David and could see that he, too, was having to make a great effort to keep from saying something rude.

At last Aunt Eva said, "So it's tonight. We'll be ready. We'll do exactly what you tell us to do, and if things go wrong, we'll never blame you."

The Rossis left soon afterward. No one thought of going to bed. Somehow it seemed harder to pack very little than to take everything. Suzy spent at least half an hour deciding which doll she would take with her, and at last fixed on a rather old one named Ada. No one could remember why the doll had been given that name but it was so long ago that this was not surprising. The new silk dress fitted her well enough. Suzy said, "I didn't make it for her but now it doesn't matter. Some other time I'll do her a better one."

Pali put his bear in the hall, next to the small bag that Aunt Eva had packed for him. The bear was the one he had had since he was born, so there was no problem of choice about that. The bag was small enough for him to carry on his shoulders. Aunt Eva had said that each person must be responsible for his or her own bag and baggage. Peter's violin case had a strap that he could hang around his shoulders, and he fixed one like it for David so that he could carry Papa's violin. Aunt Eva decided what was to go into the bags that each of them carried: underpants and undershirts—two of each—a warm jersey, a washcloth and soap, a toothbrush and toothpaste, a spare pair of trousers or a skirt if there was room for them. No nightclothes, she said. That would be a luxury.

Later, she disappeared into her own room and could be

heard scrabbling around in there, opening and shutting drawers and wardrobes and cupboards. Now and then she came out and asked, "Where are the jigsaws? The knitting needles? I can't find anything."

Then she went back without waiting for someone to answer.

"Food," she said once, when she came out. She stood in front of the refrigerator for a few minutes, picking out cheese and stale bread, crackers, a small cake, and some cooked beans, which she put in a bowl with a lid. Then she went back into her room.

Some time after midnight Mrs. Nagy came sliding in from the hall, dragging something heavy after her. David was the first to see her. In spite of himself he let out a shout, "You can't! You can't!"

She hissed, "Shut up, you stupid brat!"

At that moment Aunt Eva came out of her room. She paused at the door and said sharply, "What did you say, Mrs. Nagy?"

"Ah, there you are," Mrs. Nagy said, turning to her as if David had vanished. "I've just finished packing my things. Now I'm all ready."

"So I see."

Hearing the talk in the hall, the others came out to see what was happening. Aunt Eva stood and took a long look at Mrs. Nagy's bundle. It was a fat roll, more than three feet long and as thick as a man's body. It was wrapped in dark-blue canvas cloth and tied around with a rope, with several tight knots along its length. One end of the rope was left loose to pull it by, and there was a loop that might have served to carry the bundle with if Mrs. Nagy were a great deal bigger. Mrs. Nagy looked it over defiantly, nodding her head up and down, then said, "It's not as big as a cello. I can carry it easily."

"Suzy is leaving her cello behind," Aunt Eva pointed out, looking as if she were holding her temper with difficulty.

"She's taking her doll," Mrs. Nagy said.

There was a pause, and it seemed now that Aunt Eva was having trouble not bursting out laughing. At last she said, "Is that a doll you have in there, Mrs. Nagy?"

"No."

"Then what is it?"

"That's my business."

"I'm sorry, but it's the business of all of us. You'll have to tell me."

"Send the children away."

"No. We're all in this together."

"That one is too small." Mrs. Nagy pointed at Pali. "He shouldn't listen to adult conversation."

"It's rude to point," Pali said loudly, then went to stand beside Aunt Eva, glaring at Mrs. Nagy who glared back with her eyes narrowed.

"Age doesn't matter anymore," Aunt Eva said, and she sounded very tired. "Either you do as I say or you just can't come with us."

They measured each other and Mrs. Nagy began to say, "You can't dictate to me—" Suddenly she dropped her eyes and said in a low voice, "My rugs. My Persian rugs. I've had them all my life. They were my father's, and his father had them before that. I can't go without them."

"They're only bits of wool," Aunt Eva said gently. "The people who made them have grandchildren who know how to make more. You can get new ones when the war is over."

But it was no use. Mrs. Nagy would not say another word. She stood like a stone statue beside her bundle and simply made no answer to all Aunt Eva's pleas. One by one the children went back into their rooms to finish tidying up. Then they congregated in the living room, taking turns holding Minna, who was so pleased to be allowed in there at all that she submitted to all the different styles of petting.

The violins were ready in the hall, each case containing also some socks and underwear, so as to make the bags of clothes even smaller. Aunt Eva was to have her shopping bag, as well as one of the violins. Once or twice she paused for a moment beside Mrs. Nagy, by now sitting crouched on top of her bundle, almost as if she were about to open up the argument again. But each time she gave up the idea.

"We can't blame her," she said to the children. "She's in a state of shock. I think she didn't really believe until now that we would have to go in the end. We'll just have to put up with her."

"And her bundle?" Pali asked.

"And her bundle. It's either let her take that or leave her behind."

"Then let's leave her behind."

"No. Two wrongs don't make a right. We must always be charitable toward weaker people."

"She doesn't look weak to me," Pali said, though he knew Aunt Eva would not agree with him.

So Mrs. Nagy was the first person Mrs. Rossi saw when she came into the hall at precisely four o'clock. She gave her one quick look, then followed Aunt Eva into the living room where all the children were half dozing in the big chairs and on the sofa. Pali, who was fast asleep, woke up with a jerk. Mrs. Rossi closed the door and asked quietly, so as not to be heard in the hall, "Did you try to get her to take less? That bundle is pretty big."

"I tried but it's no use. We've made our own bundles smaller. We can throw ours away if necessary."

"What on earth has she got in it?"

"Rugs, she says, but I think she has clothes in there as well."

"Can she carry it?"

"She says she can."

"Well, we'll just have to make the best of it. We'll soon find out if she can really carry it herself. Is everyone ready?"

"Yes. How is it outside?"

"Very quiet. No one is stirring that I could see. The hardest part will be getting to where the van is parked. You all know the side streets well enough, I think. We'll have to string out a bit, and try to keep in sight of each other. If we see or hear anyone coming, we can hide in a doorway. That's more easily done if we go one by one than in a crowd."

"Will I ever see you again?"

"Don't think like that, don't talk like that. How do we know? You're going in the right direction. The first thing is to get safely into the van—one thing at a time."

"The van—how big is it? What is it like?"

"You'll see. Now we must be off. Béla will be back at six o'clock. You must be settled in before that."

"Béla?"

"The driver. I'll explain when we get there."

§ 9 §

It was creepy out on the landing in the dim light of the stairwell. Suzy held David's hand tightly, feeling her skin tingle with excitement. David felt it, too, and pressed her hand now and then to comfort her and drive off her fears. She was not really afraid, but she seemed to have developed an extra set of eyes and ears, which made every move more full of action. Softly, side by side, she and David followed the others down the four long flights of stairs. Mrs. Rossi had said that they couldn't use the elevator, since it could be heard in the apartments that were nearest to the shaft.

They stood in perfect silence while Mrs. Rossi unlocked the outer door of the building. Suzy thought she looked like a big, friendly bear in her fur coat. Aunt Eva was wearing hers, too, and had made them all put on their winter coats although the weather was already quite warm.

"Running away from danger is always a cold business," she said. "You'll be glad of those coats later."

The street was deserted and dark, except for a light at the far end where the German High Command was. A few soldiers were standing there, but they were huddled together in conversation with each other and didn't see the little group slip out into the street and around the corner. It was a cloudy night with a faint moon shining through, just enough to light their way in the side street, where there was no public lighting at all. Suzy could see Pali huddled close to Aunt Eva, clutching his bear and tilting over sideways with the weight of his shoulder bag. She whispered to David, "Silly to have brought my doll— you must think I'm an awful fool."

"Not at all," he said. "I wish I had my bear."

"Fourteen, and you still have your bear!"

"Of course. I'll have him forever. Nothing like a bear when you're feeling sad or frightened. Mind you, he's pretty worn now. His ears are bald and his neck is very thin and wobbly, but his eyes are as good as new."

"What's his name?"

"Flaubert."

Suzy giggled in the darkness, suddenly feeling much safer.

Aunt Eva and Mrs. Rossi kept close to the walls of the houses, so as to be able to slip into a doorway if necessary. The rest of them followed suit, the dark niches of the doorways at intervals along the street giving a feeling of security. Suzy knew this was not sensible, since people hiding in a doorway would be trapped if they were discovered. But there was no one there to discover them. At any other time there might have been stragglers, even at this hour of the night, but now everyone was staying at home, afraid to go out because of the curfew.

They walked through a dozen side streets, leaving the shops behind and entering the part of the city where there were warehouses and stores of all kinds. Here it was more open, and there were no doorways to hide in. Besides, the moon had sailed out from behind the clouds and seemed to be deliberately sending a strong, clear beam along the length of the streets. Still, Mrs. Rossi marched along, hurrying now as if she were feeling the need to get into cover quickly. Ahead of her Suzy saw that Pali was almost running to keep up, stopping now and then to hitch the strap of his bag up onto his shoulder. No one could help him, since they were all loaded with their own burdens. Mrs. Nagy was having trouble with her bundle, constantly shifting it from one shoulder to the other as if it were hurting her, but no one could help her, either.

At last Mrs. Rossi turned into an open graveled yard and crossed to a van that was parked in a line with some others, their tails to the outer wall. She waited until they had all come up, then moved into the space between the vans and along the side of one of them until she came to the huge steel door at the back. She rummaged in the pocket of her coat and took out a key, with which she undid the padlock that held the door shut. With a tremendous heave she lifted the door upward and outward. It made a loud grinding sound that echoed through the silent night.

"This is your house, for a while," she said, panting for breath from the strain. "You had better climb in at once. I wish the door wouldn't make that noise."

No one wanted to be the first. For some reason it looked like a trap, as if when they got inside they would never again be able to get out. Then David said, "Here goes!"

He threw his bundle onto the floor of the van and climbed up. He disappeared into the darkness inside and reappeared a moment later with a short ladder, like a ship's ladder, in his hands. He fixed it onto two hooks that were specially made to fit it, so that first Mrs. Rossi and then Aunt Eva were able to climb aboard. Peter jumped up beside David to give them a hand, and one by one the others followed, passing up their bundles first.

"We must find the flashlights," Mrs. Rossi said. "Then I'll show you your hiding place."

"Hiding place!" Aunt Eva said. "You couldn't hide a cat in here."

"Just wait. We have hidden many cats." Mrs. Rossi reached up to a shelf above the door and took down two flashlights, which she handed to Aunt Eva, saying, "You must use them very cautiously, of course—the less the better. You can imagine how clearly a light inside the van would be seen. And there is also the question of conserving the batteries. I was lucky to get four new ones. There are other rules. No one should speak or move about while the van is stationary, except at night. It will be all right when the engine is running, but when it's switched off sounds can be heard quite clearly from outside."

The moonlight through the open door showed them that the van was packed with furniture: tables, chairs, sofas, armchairs, beds, wardrobes, chests, and boxes of china and glass with labels saying what was inside them. All of these things were neatly stored, wedged against each other with the smaller things in front, so that they wouldn't slide about when the van swung from side to side. The only free space was a few feet near the door.

Mrs. Rossi pointed toward the closely packed furniture and said, "David, take the ladder and climb up there. Take one of the flashlights."

David placed the ladder firmly against a solid-looking

chest and climbed up until he was crouched on top of the range of taller pieces, under the roof of the van. Mrs. Rossi gestured to him to go farther back. Little by little he crawled along, until they saw him reach a gap between two wardrobes. He disappeared into the gap, and they could hear him drop to the floor. After a moment his head reappeared and he said in an astonished tone, "There's a little room in there. It's marvelous."

"Can we go up?" Peter asked.

"Yes, yes, come along."

Peter went up the ladder and helped Mrs. Rossi, who crawled along until she could follow David through the gap. Pali was next, then Mrs. Nagy. Suzy wondered if she would refuse, or say she couldn't climb, but she made no complaint. She crawled over the top of the furniture without a word, though she whined like a hungry dog as she went.

Suzy was the last to go. David came forward and held out a hand to help her up and she lost some of her fear as together they went through the threatening gap.

One of her earliest dreams had been of finding a secret room in their own apartment, containing all kinds of wonderful treasures. Sometimes the dream was so vivid that the memory stayed with her for days afterward. Now it seemed to have come true.

A ladder had been placed against the wardrobe so that one could climb down into the space beyond, and there it was, a room the width of the van and about seven feet deep. Three walls consisted of the front and sides of the van, with benches made of long boxes against them. On the right-hand side there was a door with a bolt and padlock. The fourth side was composed of several enormous wardrobes with their doors facing into the room. In the middle there was another box to serve as a table.

"That door on the right can only be opened from the inside of the van," Mrs. Rossi said. She pointed to the benches. "These are your beds. Not very comfortable but you won't mind for a few days. And here is your bathroom."

She opened the door of one of the wardrobes and they saw that a portable lavatory and a washbasin had been fitted inside.

"It's a miracle," Aunt Eva said. "I've never seen such a big wardrobe."

"I'm sure you haven't," Mrs. Rossi said. "It was made specially for us. Of course, you'll have to empty the bucket from time to time. You can do this at night, when the driver is away. I'll give you the key of the padlock so that you can open the door. You must be very careful about how and when you do that."

"The driver doesn't sleep in the van, then?"

"No. He has regular places where he stops, and that's when you'll be able to get out and walk about for a while."

While they were speaking, Mrs. Nagy had gone to sit in the corner, placing her bundle carefully at her feet. Her mouth was tightly shut and her eyes cast down, as if she had nothing to do with the other people crammed into the tight little room. It was clear that she was laying claim to her place. It would take courage to try to oust her, if anyone wished to do so, but in fact everyone was so pleased to see her quiet that no one would have dreamed of disturbing her.

Mrs. Rossi was opening another wardrobe, saying, "And here is your kitchen. There's a full bottle of kerosene

86

for the stove, and you should have enough for the whole journey. You'll have to be very careful not to set the van on fire, so you won't use it much—just to warm up some soup or make coffee sometimes."

"Won't the driver smell the coffee?"

"Not if you make it at night."

"It sounds as if we should sleep by day and stay awake at night."

"Most people have done that."

Aunt Eva was unpacking her stores of food, bread and cheese and cans of soup and beans. Suddenly, everyone was very still, watching her. Everything she did was as precise and determined as if she were in her own kitchen. She placed the cans and a bag of hard bread on a shelf in the tiny kitchen, saying comfortably, "You've thought of everything. There's even a little rim to keep things from falling off. I wish you could come with us, Mrs. Rossi."

"So do I. There's nothing I'd like more than to visit my people again, but I'm more useful here, and I must take care of my husband. Now, here is a list of places where you will be safe if you have to leave the van for any reason. Most of them are in Italy, I'm afraid. We still have only one safe place in Austria. This driver goes by Graz and Klagenfurt, then over the Brenner Pass and down to Bolzano. You will leave him in the mountains, near Tirano, where my cousins live. Look, I'll show you."

They sat together on one of the benches and bent over a tiny map that she had drawn, as well as a list of names and addresses written on a scrap of dark-colored paper.

"The papers are small so that you can eat them if you think they might fall into the wrong hands," Mrs. Rossi said. "The children would help."

"Has that ever happened?"

"Once only. The driver discovered the people and betrayed them."

"This driver?"

"No. We could never use that one again. Béla is new. He's not young but he hasn't got a suspicious nature. In fact, he's rather cheerful. He likes to stop here and there and drink with people he meets in the little towns and villages. This could be good for you, because you could get out then for some exercise."

"How many runs has he done?"

"This is his fifth, for us, but he doesn't know it. Now I think you should memorize the names on the list, all of you, in case of accidents."

"What kind of accidents?"

"We don't know. But if some of you were to get separated from the others for any reason, it would be good to know that you could meet again at one of these places. Just do as I say."

Poor Mrs. Rossi looked so distressed that Aunt Eva didn't ask any more questions. Instead she said, "I've heard that the mountains are beautiful."

"Yes. The Brenner is a very high pass and you may be able to get a view from up there. You can see for miles. Some of the others prefer to go by Tarvisio but Béla likes to go by the highest way."

"Where is he now?"

"Sleeping. He'll be here quite soon, at six o'clock. Now I must go. You can let me out by the door."

"How do we know the soldiers are not outside?" Mrs. Nagy asked suddenly.

"There's a peephole. Look, I'll show you."

Mrs. Nagy didn't move, but Aunt Eva went to have a closer look at the door. Sure enough, a tiny hole had been cut in the middle of the door and a small lens set into it, so that the people inside could look out but no one from the outside could look in.

"You've thought of everything," Aunt Eva said again. "I've been worrying about that since I saw the door."

"I forgot to tell you that the door can't be seen from the outside," Mrs. Rossi said. "It's made so that the lines don't show against the rest of the body of the van. Now, open the door for me and I'll be off."

Aunt Eva peered through the lens and then cautiously opened the door. The padlock and the bolt had been recently oiled, so that they opened without a sound. The moon was gone but the dawn was just beginning to light up the sky. It was good to breathe the clean morning air for a moment, while Mrs. Rossi climbed out.

"Don't be frightened when you hear me closing up the back door," she said. She moved away at once, with only a few whispered words, "Good-bye and good luck!"

Carefully, Aunt Eva closed the door and bolted and locked it. A moment later they heard the back door close with a thump that shook the whole van. For a full minute it seemed that they were in utter darkness, and then tiny rays of light trickled in through various cracks in the structure of the van.

As if by common consent, everyone sat down without a word. Even Mrs. Nagy was silent, though this was a moment when she might have begun to moan. They had not long to wait. It was no more than ten minutes later that they heard the sound of heavy boots on the gravel outside, and the sound of a man whistling. It was a cheerful sound and Suzy couldn't help feeling that there was something friendly in it. They heard the door of the cab open and the man climb inside and start up the engine. He revved it up for a few seconds, and then the van moved slowly out over the gravel and on to the smoother road outside.

§ 10 §

The sound of the engine soon turned into a quiet purr, so regular that everyone began to relax. As soon as they were out of the city the road became quite smooth, and there was no more turning of corners. They could see nothing, but a faint wind hummed around them and the air that came into the van through the various cracks smelled fresh and clean. No one wanted to move or speak, though there was no reason for silence now. Once, Aunt Eva went cautiously to the peephole and peered out but she came away shaking her head as if to say that she could see very little.

Pali was the first to go to sleep. He stretched out quietly on the bench where he had been sitting, pulled his coat around his ears, closed his eyes and seemed to fall asleep at once. Suzy was next. She was sitting beside Aunt Eva, and she just leaned against her slowly, almost as if she were going to fall off onto the floor. Aunt Eva moved gently away and laid her down, putting her bag under her head. Then Peter said softly, "They have the right idea. We've been up all night."

"Should one of us stay awake, in case the van stops or

something happens?" David asked, yawning widely at the same time.

"I'll keep watch," Aunt Eva said. "I'll only be half asleep anyway and I'd wake up if the van were to stop."

"Shouldn't you wake us if that happens?"

"I suppose so," she said doubtfully. "Would there be any danger of one of you shouting out in fear?"

"I don't think so," Peter said. "We've been frightened for so long that we're used to it by now. I never shout when I wake up."

"Neither do I," David said. "I wake up with a jerk, but I don't make a noise."

"Some people who never shouted have begun to do it now," Aunt Eva said. "It takes people in lots of ways."

"I'd like to be wide-awake if there's danger," Peter said firmly. "I don't like surprises."

"Very well, then. I'll call you when we stop."

Peter and David both lay on the floor. Mrs. Nagy looked at them for a moment, then placed her roll carefully on the bench and lay down with her head on it. Before he fell asleep, David saw her lift herself up on one elbow and heard her say quietly to Aunt Eva, "Do you think they'll stay asleep? You don't think one of them might get up and start rooting around after a while?"

Aunt Eva gave a long, hissing sigh, then said, "Really, Mrs. Nagy, you go very far. Don't you trust anyone at all?"

"No," Mrs. Nagy said after a moment, "I don't. I know boys. They're always up to pranks, teasing an old woman. They think it's funny, I suppose."

"How old are you, by the way?" Aunt Eva asked.

"Never mind. Why do you ask?"

"I think I'm about ten years older than you, that's why."

"It's not very nice to boast."

"A fact is a fact," Aunt Eva said. "I see no point in covering up something that anyone can find out if they want to. Besides, not many people would boast of being old. I think it's more the other way around, that they try to conceal their age."

That was the end of the conversation. Mrs. Nagy lay down again and closed her eyes. Good old Aunt Eva, David thought before he fell asleep. Even now she hadn't lost her common sense. By not asking what Mrs. Nagy was afraid of, she had managed to get her on the wrong foot. She would be quiet now for quite a while.

When the first stop came, there was no need for Aunt Eva to waken them. First there was a long grinding noise from the brakes, then a series of small jerks as the van came to a halt. Every eye popped open, every head lifted. Aunt Eva put her finger on her lips but this was not necessary. No one would have said a word. David felt his skin crawl with sweat. He glanced at his watch and saw that it was noon, though he had had no idea that they had slept so long. His head felt heavy and sore. He could see that Suzy was watching him and he tried to send her a reassuring smile, but he knew that she must see how scared he was.

Then they heard the driver open his door and jump to the ground, and a moment later he was walking away, whistling the same tune. David recognized it now as a Hungarian mountain song, and he felt thankful that the driver was not one of those people who sang and whistled the German marching songs, as so many did. It was true that they were wonderful songs, with a great rhythm and swing to them, but David had heard the soldiers sing them so often that he still found them threatening.

Aunt Eva stood up quietly and went to look through the peephole. After what seemed an age she came back and said quietly, "We're at a café. I could just see the sign. There are several trucks lined up, as if all the drivers are in having something to eat. I think we could safely do the same."

"I want to go to the lavatory," Pali whispered.

"Can you wait until we're moving again?"

"No."

"Then go. Be very quiet."

"It's like school," Mrs. Nagy said with a disagreeable smile. "We all have to ask permission to go to the lavatory."

"Yes," Aunt Eva said cheerfully. "Or you could decide to get out and walk to Italy, if you like that better and if you know the way. Now it's time to eat."

The meal of bread and cheese tasted heavenly, and there was a piece of cake for each of them afterward. Mrs. Nagy took hers without a word of thanks, turning it over and over in her hands as if to emphasize that she found it very small.

"We'll have to tighten our belts," Aunt Eva said sharply. "We don't know how long we'll be on the road. It was only possible to take so much."

Mrs. Nagy made no reply but she had a new, satisfied look, as if she were hoping that Aunt Eva's nerve was about to break. How good it would be to open the door and put her outside, and let her walk, as Aunt Eva had suggested! David found it was better not to look at her. It would be a disaster if she noticed that she was being watched. She would really love to have another grievance.

After they had eaten, the room felt very narrow. The floor on which they had slept so well was suddenly as hard as a rock and the windowless walls seemed to close in around them. Every movement outside the van made them glare around wildly. Pali began to look smaller and smaller, huddled into his coat as if he were cold, though in fact it was rather too warm now that the air had stopped circulating. With a sick feeling, David realized that a cough or a sneeze could be a disaster. Perhaps the others had thought of the same thing. No one moved or spoke.

At last they heard the driver come back, shouting good-byes to his companions. Then he was whistling his way up into the cab again and starting the engine, and they were off.

Aunt Eva began very quietly to take things out of her bag.

"We must occupy ourselves as much as possible," she said. "Otherwise we'll go crazy from boredom. I know what you're all thinking of."

"Music," Peter said. "I wish I could practice. This is my time for it every day."

"And mine," Suzy said. "I feel fidgety when I don't practice."

"So do I, so do I," the other two said.

"And I should be cooking dinner," Aunt Eva said, "or making bread. We'll have to think of different occupations now. We can exchange them tomorrow, if we want to."

She had a pad of drawing paper and several pencils for Pali, a book of crossword puzzles and a miniature chess-board, as well as dominoes for the others. For herself she had a pack of cards.

parts of their box, and by shielding them with their hands whenever they began to fall over.

"Check," Mrs. Nagy said softly.

David couldn't help exclaiming, "Well done!"

She straightened her back and gave him a pleased smile. Then he had to concentrate on how to handle her move and the game went on. At last he said apologetically, "Checkmate, I think."

She gave a long look at the board, then said, "You're right. It's mate." She let out a long breath. "You're a fine chess player already. I like playing with you."

"Thank you. You're a very good player yourself."

"I like the way you don't pause too long before moving your pieces. My father always said that if you couldn't plan your move within ten minutes, you should find some other game to play."

It was the first time she had ever been civil to him, but David concealed his surprise, saying, "I usually see what I want to do quite quickly but I'm afraid to move without studying the board again, in case I'm making a mistake."

"Quite right. It's always better to be certain. Now we'll have another game."

He won the next game, too, and still she didn't fly out at him. He knew by the way Aunt Eva glanced at them from time to time with a little smile that she was pleased. When they had finished the second game she said, "That's enough chess. Variety is the spice of life."

At that moment they all felt the brakes being put on, and slowly the van came to a halt. No one moved or spoke, but their wild eyes revealed what everyone was thinking: This is the moment; it's all finished. Aunt Eva whispered unnecessarily, "Don't move."

98

They stared at the wall of the van as if they hoped to see through it. They could hear the driver jump to the ground and run around to the back. As still as mice, they heard him fumble with the lock, then rattle it. They had left no clue, Peter thought. He had looked carefully before climbing over the stacked furniture. He recalled every detail clearly, as if he could see, and knew that they had left no telltale scrap of paper, no trailing thread of cloth.

Then they heard the driver move away from the door, as if he had decided against opening it. Aunt Eva stood up very quietly and slid toward the peephole, where she stayed motionless for several minutes before creeping back to her place and sitting down. She said not a word and there was no way of knowing what she had seen. Soundlessly, Pali picked up his pencil and paper and began to draw. No one else moved.

Voices broke the eerie silence, the driver shouting, "I thought you were all asleep in there! Do you think I run this wagon on buttermilk?" Another voice answered loudly, grumpily, "Coming, coming! Don't eat us! Why aren't you stopping off for the night?"

"I want to get over the border first."

"I wouldn't advise it," the other said. "You'd be crossing in pitch darkness. And the soldiers are always in a bad humor at night, poking into everything. My advice is that you stop a mile down the road in the village tonight and be off at first light in the morning."

A splashing sound and rhythmic pounding told them that someone was filling the fuel tank. Then the driver said, "Maybe you're right. Is there a good pull-in?"

"Couldn't be better, a field in front of the inn. They won't be asleep yet."

"How do you know?"

"It belongs to my sister, that's why." There was a pause while he replaced the cap on the fuel tank. "I haven't seen you this way before—you from Budapest?"

"Yes. I pass now and then, when I have a load."

"What are you carrying?"

"Furniture for some officer. They move like snails, with all their property. Well, I must be off. Good night to you."

"Good night. Call again when you're passing."

The driver crunched his way back to the cab and climbed in, then moved off slowly. Aunt Eva shook her head to indicate that it was still not safe to speak. Sure enough, after a mile or so they heard the brakes again, and the van made a wide turn and halted.

§ 11 §

This time, there was a long silence after the driver had locked up and left the van. No one wanted to be the first to move, though they could hear no sound from outside. Everyone was looking at Aunt Eva. She sat tensely, like a watching cat, staring in front of her, as if this concentration would help her to hear more. Perhaps it did. After a few moments she said, "I think we can open the door. I'll go first."

Breathing in the fresh air was like taking a long drink of cool springwater. It filled the cramped room, and the rank stuff they had been breathing was washed out like soapsuds. They all filled their lungs deeply, several times, as if they had been drowning and had suddenly surfaced. From outside, Aunt Eva said softly, "You can come out. It's wonderful out here."

Peter went first and helped Mrs. Nagy down, then Suzy followed, with David close behind, and last of all Pali. They stood in a row, backs to the van, afraid to move, until Aunt Eva said again, "It's wonderful. There's no one. Run, run!"

They were on the edge of a huge field bordered with

trees, still quite bare though leaves had begun to show here and there on the low bushes that grew in between. The van had been parked so that the side with the secret door opened on to the field. Peering around the corner, Peter saw the inn at a little distance. All its shutters were up and lights showed dimly through the chinks. A high, sailing moon lit up the sky so that the whole scene was as clear as daylight. Apart from the inn there seemed to be no houses near, though he could see the lights of a village a few hundred yards away.

Suddenly he began to run like a young horse, wildly, taking off toward the middle of the field, stretching his legs as hard as he could, pounding up and down and throwing back his shoulders while his elbows crooked themselves against his sides. The others followed, except for Mrs. Nagy and Aunt Eva who stayed close to the van. He glanced back and saw them walking quickly to and fro. Then he gave himself up to the most delicious sensation in the world, feeling the cramped muscles ease themselves free of the tensions of the day.

At last he threw himself on the grass and lay spread out, his arms and legs wide, staring at the sky. The others arrived and joined him in a row, savoring the minutes of freedom one by one, until at last David said, "We should go back. Someone might see us."

Reluctantly, they clambered upright and went back toward the van. Aunt Eva had got out things to eat but she said, "Better to eat standing up, outside. We'll be long enough in there, later. We're lucky to have the moonlight."

When they had finished she said briskly, "Now we must dig a hole and bury the contents of the chemical toilet.

This is a wonderful place for it—couldn't have been better, in fact."

"I'll have nothing to do with it," Mrs. Nagy said in a venomous whisper.

"It's usually men's work," Aunt Eva said calmly. "If you don't want to watch, you can take a walk."

"I certainly will," she said, and stalked off along the edge of the field.

"She's a funny one," Aunt Eva said tolerantly. "She doesn't mind a bit making use of it when she feels the need—ordering everyone away from the door and making such a business of her rights. You'd learn a lot, just by watching her."

"How do we dig a hole?" Peter asked.

"With the spade. You must have seen it in the lavatory, in the corner."

"Yes, but I didn't know what it was for."

Together, she and Peter dug a deep hole by the hedge and emptied the bucket into it. Then they put in some fresh grass before mixing in more of the disinfectant. Peter asked in amazement, "How do you come to know so much? I would have no idea how to do these things."

"Experience, I suppose. My grandmother lived in the country, on a farm. They had plenty of land but they didn't have indoor plumbing. We would have been delighted to have anything as modern as this article. You find out as life goes on that there are many things you can live without. I must say, though, that I'm very fond of modern plumbing."

"Poor Mrs. Nagy!" Peter said suddenly. "She doesn't seem able to put up with anything nasty. She doesn't seem to enjoy anything either."

"Except chess," Aunt Eva said. "She looked happy while she was playing with David."

"Because she hoped she'd beat him, I suppose."

"No, just happy. Each of us has at least one thing that makes us feel happy. We're lucky to have a number of those things."

"I wish I had your wisdom."

"No hurry. You will, some day."

"Do you think Papa and Mama will ever come back?"

"That's in the hands of God."

"What is God doing for us?"

"It's not our business to inquire. He knows we're here."

"Does he?"

"Yes. He hears us and watches over us. We must pray, all the time, if we're to be saved."

"Do you pray?"

"Yes, a lot. Haven't you noticed?"

"Is that what you're doing when you sit quietly for a long time without moving?"

"Of course. I know now that by next Sabbath we'll be safe in Italy."

"And Papa and Mama?"

"That's something else. I pray for them, too."

But Peter could see that she had little or no hope for them. He also saw that it would be wrong to try to pin her down about this. He found now that he didn't want to know what she thought. Part of her wisdom was that she didn't express all of her thoughts. That was the main difference between her and Mrs. Nagy, who seemed to say everything that came into her head.

Having slept so much during the day, no one wanted to go to bed. They sat for a long time with the secret door open and the moonlight streaming in. The tiny space had almost begun to feel like a home, with a place for each person. Pali was hugging his bear and Suzy's doll was beside her on the bench, though she was not giving it as much attention as she would have done at home. Almost overnight, Peter thought, she had acquired a grown-up look. The observation gave him a little burst of satisfaction—she would be his ally and helper now, instead of a dependent. It occurred to him that he had never had a real conversation with her. He would begin tomorrow. There was plenty of time.

When the moonlight began to fade, Aunt Eva locked the door and they lay down and slept. It was so quiet that a passing owl's hoot seemed like the whistle of a train. Then either that owl or another one landed on the metal roof of the van and they could hear its claws scrabbling and rattling as it tried to keep a foothold. A flock of bats squeaked for a while before moving on.

Trickles of daylight were seeping in when they heard the driver coming back. He checked the back door, as he had done the night before, shaking the handle vigorously so that everyone woke up. Then he marched around to the front and climbed up into the cab and they were off. Now it all began to feel familiar, as if they had been living like this all their lives. There was stale bread and cheese for breakfast, and then David and Mrs. Nagy played chess again while Aunt Eva played patience.

Peter's fingers itched to take out his violin and practice. The very idea of doing this made him laugh out loud. But there was nothing to stop him from thinking about it, and as he knew from experience, a great deal of the work of practicing was done during the thinking time. Quietly now, while Suzy laid out the dominoes, he began to go through the Beethoven concerto, from the four drumbeats at the beginning of the accompaniment to the moment when the violin plays the opening split chords that soar upward quietly, until the first theme comes forward.

He had been told that he could play the concerto with the orchestra at the next concert. Now it would be Janos Varga, probably. That would be all right. Janos was a good friend of Peter's and had always defended him when some of the others were spiteful about his being a Jew. They were funny about that—they seemed to think that he had some unfair advantage, because he had inherited a natural talent. Peter had felt badly about it until one of his teachers told him it was the same all over the world, not only for Jews but for all kinds of other people. In the end, it was impossible to tell who was the ideal person—someone striped, perhaps. But mixed people seemed to be suspected by absolutely everyone.

The idea came to him that he might never play that concerto now, or even that he might never play anything, ever again. He glanced over at Aunt Eva and saw that she was watching him. Then she turned her eyes down to her cards again and for the first time he noticed that she was not really looking at them at all. Now he knew, from what she had said last night, that she was praying.

The day dragged on and everyone began to look sleepy. Pali closed his drawing papers into their cover and lay down. Immediately, they all followed suit. They slept again, soothed now by the hum of the engine, quietly taking them to safety.

Once, there was a long stop and a confusion of voices

as if they were near a café or a garage. Peter and David were the first to wake up, but a moment later Aunt Eva and Suzy were awake, too. They stayed perfectly still, watching each other, though none of them could make out what was happening. Presently the van moved on again, but slowly, and there was more conversation. Then someone shouted, *"Alles in Ordnung!"* Soon after that the van moved on, gradually gathering speed.

Much later, Peter felt it sway gently, like a cradle, as if it had begun to climb a mountain road with many curves. Once they were in the mountains, Mrs. Rossi had said, most of the risk of discovery would be over.

No longer alert for danger, Peter was surprised to be awakened by a series of grinding bumps and a sudden swerve of the van, as if it were being pulled in suddenly to the side of the road. In the dim light he could see that everyone else had been awakened, too. He peered at his watch and saw that it was just after five o'clock. The engine pounded in an unhealthy way for a few seconds, then stopped. No one moved. They heard the driver open the door of the cab and jump down to the ground. He seemed to be walking all around the van. Perhaps it was a flat tire. But surely that would have tilted the van sideways. At the front, again, the driver lifted the cover of the engine and threw it back noisily.

Aunt Eva moved softly to the peephole and looked through it, but she came back shaking her head to indicate that she hadn't been able to see anything useful. It was clear that she was really worried, that this was something she had not anticipated. When she glanced from one of them to the other, one could see that she was estimating how each individual would behave in a crisis and sending a silent warning that they were to follow her lead if necessary.

There was complete silence outside. It seemed that other trucks were not using this road, or else they had all finished their runs and gone into a village inn for the night. Peter signaled to Aunt Eva that he would like to look out, and she nodded after a moment's thought. It was terrifying to move but he did it so quietly and slowly that he was sure no one outside could have been aware of it. At the peephole he leaned forward until he could place his right eye against it. Then, without a sound, he seemed to freeze into a block of stone.

There, quite close to the van, exactly in front of the secret door and gazing directly at it, was the driver. He seemed to be staring at Peter, though he couldn't possibly have seen him. He was a short, fat man of middle age, with curly gray hair. He was wearing blue overalls, and a blue cloth cap was on the back of his head. His big gray eyes looked anxious, as if he were uncertain what to do. Then, as Peter watched, he moved closer to the side of the van and said softly, "Open the door. I'm afraid you'll have to come out."

There was nothing for it but to obey. Peter turned to Aunt Eva and said, "He knows we're here. He wants me to open the door."

"I heard him. You had better do as he says."

She got up quickly and came to stand beside him. The others remained perfectly still, watching. Slowly, Peter pulled back the bolt and pressed down the lever that held the door shut. Then he pushed the door open very slightly.

It moved quite silently on its oiled hinges. There was no point in putting off the moment of confrontation any longer. With one long sweep he opened the door right back and jumped down to the ground.

They were parked on the grassy verge of a road that wound upward and upward into the mountains. Stunted bushes alternated with stretches of pine forest. The carpet of dead ferns from last year was beginning to show spots of brilliant green where the new shoots appeared. To the right the land rose steeply and to the left it dropped away almost perpendicularly, so that the road appeared to be clinging precariously to the mountainside. There was no sign of a house or of any life, not even a sheep grazing.

Peter turned and helped Aunt Eva to the ground. Now the others were crowded in the doorway, all except Mrs. Nagy. He had no time to think of her. The driver had stepped back a little, the better to see them, perhaps.

"Five of you!" he said softly.

"Six," Aunt Eva said. "There's another one inside."

There was a short silence. The driver seemed bewildered, unable to speak. Then he said, "I thought there might be two—but six!"

"I'm sorry," Aunt Eva said. "We couldn't leave anyone behind."

"The engine has broken down," he said roughly. "I'll have to get it fixed."

"How?"

"There's a mountain village a few miles back. I saw it when we passed through. There must be a mechanic there. I can't take you with me."

"Are you saying we must get out?"

"How can I keep you? The mechanic would find you in two shakes. He might have the van up on the lift. It's out of the question."

"The children—"

"No one is a child, these days. No one makes any distinction."

"Don't you?"

"Of course I do. Don't try to trap me. What can I do?"

"You could leave us here and pick us up on your way when you have the van mended."

For the first time he looked at her directly, before he said, "You mightn't survive. It might take three days. The weather is cold. There are wolves—bears, too, I've heard. Let me think."

There was dead silence while he walked away from them and seemed to have a long conversation with himself, waving his hands, shaking his head, stamping his feet as if he were arguing a case. Suddenly he whirled around and marched back.

"One possibility might work. The parish priest."

"Where?"

Aunt Eva looked around as if she thought he might be sitting in a bush somewhere quite close.

"Down in the village," the driver said, "or rather, just outside it, beside his church. I saw the house. He might be a good Christian."

"Doesn't that mean he would hate Jews?" Mrs. Nagy, of course, poking her head out above Pali's head to add her piece of mischief.

"You can stay here if you want," the driver said furiously. "A good Christian loves everyone. Make up your minds. I can't wait all evening."

"Don't mind her," Pali said. "She's nasty about everything."

The driver gave a chuckle and said, "Is that so? What's your name?"

"Pali."

"A good Hungarian name." He turned back to Aunt Eva saying, "I think you would be all right with the priest. I don't know for certain but I've heard of a few of them who have done good turns for people like you before. What do you say?"

He looked from Aunt Eva to Peter, ignoring Mrs. Nagy who had pulled back into the shadow of the van.

"We're very grateful," Aunt Eva said. "We don't want to cause trouble. Someone in the village might inform on us."

"I think not," the driver said. "Mountain people are rather more independent than city people." He turned to Peter. "What do you say, young man?"

"Yes, of course, we'll do as you say," Peter said. "We trust you completely."

"I don't know why you should, but it's true that you're as safe with me as you would be with anyone. Now, our main problem is to get back down to the village again. We'll run down on the brakes. It's the only way. You two boys can help me to turn the van."

§ 12 §

The driver got into the cab, leaving the door wide open.

"I think the road is wide enough for the turn," he called out. "If not, you'll have to go around and push from the front after a while, so that I can reverse. Do you understand what I'm saying?"

"Yes, of course."

"Then you can begin."

He slammed the door shut. Peter and David went around to the back of the van and were preparing to give the first shove when they heard Mrs. Nagy shouting, "What about me? Are you going to kill me? Push me down the mountain? Let me out! Let me out!"

"Come out, then," Aunt Eva said. "Here, take my hand. If you shout loud enough, those bears he was talking about might come out of the woods and eat us all."

"Bears! Did he say bears?"

"Yes, but I don't believe him. Now, don't start getting excited. Perhaps you should begin to walk down the road."

"Oh, very well."

"I'll go with you," Aunt Eva said. "We'll only be in the way here. You can come, too, Pali, if you like."

"No, thank you," Pali said politely. "I'd rather stay with the others."

They were ready to begin. David and Peter took the middle positions and the two smaller ones were on the outside. Heaving with all their strength, at first it seemed that the van would be too heavy for them. The driver turned the steering wheel slowly, calling instructions to them through the open door. Then they felt the first tiny movement. Again and again they heaved, until the wheels were making bigger and bigger turns, and at last there was a great moment when the van went around in a curve and began to slide off down the hill. The driver braked and waited for them to come running around to speak to him.

"I'll pick up the old ones on the way," he said. "You can follow me."

Then he was off. A hundred yards down the hill they saw him pause and let Mrs. Nagy and Aunt Eva climb in beside him.

"A good thing Mrs. Nagy is afraid to box your ears, Pali," David said. "I thought she would do it when you said she's nasty about everything. I wouldn't risk it again, if I were you."

"I shouldn't have said anything," Pali said. "Aunt Eva thinks she can't help being like that, but I bet she could improve if she put her mind to it."

"It's probably too late," Peter said. "Papa said that after a certain age, people don't want to improve. I suppose they get tired of working on themselves."

Keeping the van in sight, they trotted easily down the hill. The driver was clearly afraid to go fast, since he was depending on the brakes to hold the weight of the van. They were just behind when he turned into a grassy space in front of the priest's house. As he had said, it was right beside the church, with only the graveyard in between. The garden was fenced with light rails of wood and closed by a small iron gate, beyond which a graveled path led to the front door. The driver jumped down.

"Around to the side of the house, everyone," he said in a low voice. "Keep out of sight. You two ladies can be ready to come forward. Keep to the front. I'll explain everything to the priest. I just hope he's at home."

The windows all shone blindly in the evening sun. Still, it was agony to flit up the path and around the corner. Their hearts were pounding and they huddled close to each other as they listened for the driver's voice. First they heard him knock loudly on the front door. Then there was a sickening pause while he waited. He knocked again, just as they could hear the door being opened.

"Is the priest at home?" they heard him ask in Hungarian; and a woman's voice answered in the same language, but with a strange accent, "Yes. Who are you?"

"Up from Budapest with my van. Engine trouble."

"The priest is not an engineer."

"I don't need him for that. It's something else altogether."

"You needn't have knocked so loud."

"I'm sorry. I thought you hadn't heard me."

"The priest is at his prayers."

"He would say that life is a prayer."

There was a short pause and then she said, "You had better come in."

That was the last for what seemed a very long time. No one moved. Tall withered weeds were growing against the house, and they could hear the insects moving in them.

Something seemed to be sliding toward them through the grass.

"Snakes!" Mrs. Nagy hissed.

"Nonsense," Aunt Eva said. "It's too high for them. They go for warm places."

"You know a lot," Mrs. Nagy said bitterly.

"It's handy to know about snakes," Aunt Eva said. "Now keep quiet, if you please."

Pali thought of saying that it was probably a rat, to see what she would do. Then he wanted to giggle but he made sure not to make a sound. With the sun gone down it had begun to be very cold. Now he began to wish they could all be together inside the van. It hadn't been cold in there. He leaned close against Suzy and was glad when she put her arm around him. Then David put his arm around Suzy so that all three of them warmed each other.

Tall pines grew behind the house, all the way up the mountainside. Darkness began to stretch down like long fingers from the trees, very slowly, until it almost covered the little garden. At last they heard the door open and a strange voice talking urgently to the driver in Hungarian.

"Bring them in. They must be frozen. It will be all right. I'm sorry she kept you waiting. My housekeeper tries to save me trouble. I would have come down at once if I had known you were here. Where are they?"

"Just here."

The driver was first around the corner of the house, followed closely by the priest in his long black cassock. He was tall and bony, like a mountain horse. His black hair stood up in a bush all around his head. By now it was too dark to see his face.

115

Aunt Eva came forward, saying, "We're a nuisance, I'm afraid, but we have to think of the children."

"Of course. Don't apologize. I'm glad to see you here. You've come to the right place."

"You think it's safe?"

"As safe as anywhere these days. We don't see much company up here. I'll warn the people in the village to keep off strangers, if any of them come. They'll know what to do."

"How close are we to the village?"

"It begins just around the bend of the road, a few hundred yards away. Not a soul there would betray you. Now, come inside. You need some coffee."

"Thank you, we'll be glad of it."

Now the darkness was a blessing as they hurried toward the door of the house. It opened straight into a big room with a dining table in the middle and chairs ranged around. A bare staircase went up out of one corner. Against the far wall there was a sideboard made of some dark wood, with two brass candlesticks on it, each made to hold three candles. Only one candle in each was lit. Shelves of books filled the alcoves at either side of the huge fireplace, and there were two armchairs.

"Sit here," the priest said to Aunt Eva. "I'll light the fire at once. You must be cold."

He led Mrs. Nagy and Aunt Eva to the armchairs. Mrs. Nagy sat down at once. The priest bent to put a match to the fire, which was already laid with kindling and logs. It blazed up immediately and filled the room with a comfortable glow. Then he turned back to them and said, "Now, everyone sit down. Agnes! Coffee and bread,

116

quickly. Some cake if you have it, and milk. There are six more."

A large woman appeared in the doorway and stared at them, then said, "Six more! Glory be to God!" She turned back into the kitchen.

Aunt Eva said, "I'll help you."

She followed the housekeeper into the kitchen where they could be heard talking to each other, Aunt Eva very quietly, Agnes with little shrieks of amazement. They came back with bread and coffee and some small cakes on a tray. When the driver saw that Agnes went back into the kitchen, he carried his cup in there, too.

The priest said, "He tells me that you've been two nights on the road already."

"Yes," Aunt Eva said. "We have no idea of how long it takes. Béla seems to have done this before, for other people. He knows all about it. We thought it was a secret even from him but we were wrong."

"He's a good man. Not everyone would take risks for you when he might be in trouble himself."

"What about the mechanic?"

"He won't come up here. You should be all right so long as no one sees you."

"There are so many of us."

"That's a difficulty but we've succeeded before with a group like yours."

"Then you're doing this all the time?"

"Not as much as we'd like to," the priest said. "There isn't much we can do unless someone drops in as you did."

Before going down to the village the driver told them that they must take all of their things out of the van.

"If someone gets curious and starts poking in at the back, I can be as surprised as anyone, so long as you haven't left anything behind," he said. "Better not to leave crumbs, either."

It was quite dark by the time they began to empty the van. The priest held a lantern for them, and one by one they put their original bundles together and carried them into the house. Mrs. Nagy was the first, lugging her roll upstairs before anyone else. She made Pali stand in the hall and hold the candle for her. When she came down, she went to sit by the fire with her back to the door and seemed to make a point of not looking at anyone. When Aunt Eva went out again to brush the floor of the van she didn't offer to help.

"If she would even hold the candle as I did for her," Pali muttered to Peter.

She heard him, of course, and snapped at once, "What's that you said?"

"I just thought it's your turn to hold the candle for us. It's so dark on the stairs."

"Well, I can't. My bones are aching. I've got to keep warm."

Agnes heard this and came out of the kitchen, and stood on the stairs holding the candle, while they went up with their little packs of clothes and the two violins.

There were four rooms upstairs, each with two huge iron beds. Agnes showed them into three of the rooms, pointing out the priest's room to one side at the front. Her own home was close by, she said, and she came in by the day to look after him. Mrs. Nagy had taken possession of the other front room, and they put Aunt Eva's and Suzy's things in one of the back rooms. The three boys would share the remaining room. Peter and David went outside again to give the van a push on its way down the hill. Pali sat on the bed and leaned back to lie at full length.

"This is heaven," he said. "I wish we could stay here forever."

When they went to bed an hour or so later, he was glad to have the other two with him. The dark forest looked in at the uncurtained window. The candle flame made a tiny spot of color but all the rest was shiny blackness where anything or anyone could lurk. With the windows tightly shut, there was no sound of night birds or any of the little noises that had surrounded the parked van. Pali buried his head under the blankets and shut his eyes fiercely, hugging his bear and willing himself to go to sleep before the others did. He knew by the way they looked at each other in the dim light that they were nervous, too, but they were too old to say so.

It all looked different in the morning. Pali awoke to dim daylight, with a thick mist covering the trees that grew close to the window. Gradually, this cleared off and streaks of sunlight began to show through between the trunks. Downstairs, he found that Agnes had already arrived and was getting ready to milk the cow.

"I didn't know you had a cow," Pali said in amazement. "She didn't make any noise."

"Not everyone makes noise," Agnes said. "Of course we have a cow. How else would we get milk?"

She showed him where the cow was waiting, outside her shed, and let him have a try at milking her.

"You'll be good at it," she said, "but it would take too long to let you do it now. The cow would get impatient."

As if she knew what was being said, the cow turned her

big, pale head and fixed her eyes on him. Pali sighed deeply and said, "I wish we could stay. I'd love to have a cow."

"Perhaps there will be one where you're going."

"Perhaps."

He helped Agnes carry in the milk, strain it through a muslin cloth, and carry two jugs of it to the table for breakfast. There was no sign of Béla. The priest came in from saying Mass in the church and said, "He's supervising the repairs. It's the transmission. The mechanic thinks he can do it quickly if he can get the part he needs. It's hard to get parts for engines these days."

"Where will he get it?"

"There are Germans in the town, half an hour's drive away. They'll do things for him when they hear that he's moving an officer's furniture."

"He'll draw them on us! They'll come up and find us!" Mrs. Nagy looked wildly around the table.

The priest said soothingly, "No, he won't. Now, please don't worry more than you have to. After breakfast you should all go for a walk up the hill. You can see the whole countryside from there."

Mrs. Nagy subsided with a whimper. Aunt Eva tried to persuade her to take the priest's advice but it was no use. Nothing would persuade her to go outside. When the others set off to walk up through the trees, she retreated to her room and stayed there the whole morning.

§13§

There had been a light rain, so that the air outside was clean and fresh and scented with pine. Once they were in the forest they walked in single file. A carpet of pine needles and thin, new grass made the going soft and easy. Sometimes they had to climb over a fallen tree whose roots were surrounded by young ferns. The fronds were curled tightly, like a baby's fist, though some had begun to open out. Above them, the branches of the pines made a faint roaring sound in the wind, while down on the ground it was quite still. Here and there, as they climbed, they came to a clearing where the loggers had been at work before the winter. At one of these clearings they sat down to rest on the trunk of a tree.

"Let's thank God for this," Aunt Eva said after a moment.

"And that Mrs. Nagy stayed behind," Pali said. "She'll poison herself with her own tongue one of these days, if she's not careful."

"Now, now, you've been very good, Pali," Aunt Eva said. "Just keep it up a little longer."

"I'll try, I suppose. I wonder what she has in that bundle of hers."

"Just keep on wondering. It's not our business."

"We'll have to get back in the van with her. Can't you ask her to be more cheerful?"

"It wouldn't be any use. Glum people don't want to change."

"But why is she glum? Surely she's no worse off than the rest of us."

"I don't know why. Now that you ask, perhaps I should try to find out. There could be a reason. I know she's a lonely person."

"That's because she's nasty."

"Oh, let's forget about her!" David said. "Come on, Suzy—I'm going to run!"

He sprang off the log and began to run up the hill. Suzy leaped up at once and followed him. David kept well ahead and Suzy panted, laughing, after him, sometimes half falling, coming down on her hands and knees, then getting up again to catch up with him. At last they reached another clearing and threw themselves on the grass on their backs, looking up through the branches at the cloudless blue sky.

"I didn't know you had such long legs," Suzy said when she had her breath back. "It's like following a deer."

They sat up and looked down to where the others were still resting on the log. As they watched, first Aunt Eva and then the other two stood up and began to climb the slope toward them. Farther down they could see the roof of the priest's house and the little spire of the church, and now for the first time they caught a glimpse of the village. The houses were huddled together, only their red roofs showing.

"A pity we can't go down there," David said. "It looks like a good place. I wouldn't mind living in a village like that some day."

"Neither would I," Suzy said. "To be right on the edge of the forest would be just heavenly. I wonder if the people come up here for walks sometimes."

"We certainly will, if we ever manage to live anywhere like this."

"Aunt Eva says we'll escape."

"I love her," David said. "She's so good to everyone, and she makes me feel that I'm not just an extra nuisance."

Beyond the village they could see right down into the valley, with the road on which they had driven winding and snaking its way downward. When it reached the valley floor, it straightened out and was lost in mist.

"Come on," Suzy said suddenly. "They'll catch up with us if we don't move."

Now it seemed to her that being alone with David was the most important thing in the world. It was as if a string had tightened between them in the last few minutes, pulling them close together. He turned once to look at her and she knew that he was thinking the same. They were not running now because the slope was too steep, but the wide grassy path made by the loggers continued right to the top of the tree line.

"It would take too long to get up there," David said presently. "We'd better go back."

It was colder at this height, so that it was pleasant to walk carefully downhill until they caught up with the rest of the party. Roots of old trees were everywhere and tiny new trees had been planted or had seeded themselves in the open spaces.

Suddenly, David stopped dead. "I know!" he said. "We're in Austria. We must be. There are no mountains like these on the borders of Austria and Hungary. We must have crossed the border yesterday, during one of those stops. Do you remember the one where we heard all the talking? I thought it was a stop for fuel at a garage."

"Yes, I remember, I was half asleep. I was afraid to breathe until we were on the move again." She paused, not wanting to ask the question, then went on, "Do you think it's worse or better to be in Austria?"

"Much the same," David said. "At least we're in the mountains, and the priest will watch out for us. On the whole, I think it may be better. The Austrians like the Hungarians, I've always heard. Perhaps that's why they've learned our language."

"They mightn't think of us as Hungarians. No one seems to, these days. All the same, I wish we could stay here forever."

But the priest said this would not be safe. When they were sitting around the table after lunch he brought up the question himself.

"This village looks out of the way but in fact it's on the main road to Italy. People are always passing by and strangers often drop in to talk to me. They see the church and they guess that this is the priest's house. It's all right to risk it for a while but for a long stay you need a much quieter place."

"I think we're going to one," Aunt Eva said. "I doubt if there's a real road into that village in the mountains, where Mrs. Rossi's relatives live."

"We might even be able to play some music there."

124

"I saw you bringing in violins," the priest said. "I play sometimes, too."

"The violin?"

"Yes. I was almost going to be a professional musician but I turned into a priest instead."

"Where did you study?"

"Vienna, a long time ago. I come from a village on the border between Austria and Hungary, so I could just as easily have studied in Budapest. Agnes comes from the same village, by the way. I still practice when I get time."

"Then we're in Austria now," David said. "I guessed that we were."

"Of course. We're not too far from Graz—that would be the nearest big city but people around here hardly ever go there."

Suddenly Peter asked, "I wonder if it would be safe for us to practice? Do you think anyone would hear us?"

"Of course they would hear you, if they were anywhere near enough, but they would think it was I who was playing. They'd probably pay no attention. Do you want to practice?"

"More than anything. I could go into the woods, if you think I should. I've often done that when we were on vacations and Papa thought people mightn't like to hear us."

"Who else plays?"

"I do," Pali said, "but I'm not as good as Peter yet."

Mrs. Nagy had been looking from one of them to the other during this conversation, without making any comment but getting more and more agitated. Now she said, "That noise—it will be heard all over the country. You'll draw the Germans on us. I know how it penetrates. I've lived next to it and suffered it for years."

"You could go out into the woods while they play," the priest said kindly. "That would be the easiest solution. You'll be quite safe out there."

"The bears—the wolves—"

"Who told you those stories? Yes, there are occasional wolves but usually they avoid people."

"Usually!"

She made no more complaints, and in the late afternoon Peter went upstairs and got out the violins, to make sure that they had come to no harm. They were perfect, lying like sleeping babies in their cases. It felt good to pick up his and try out a few notes on it before starting to walk up and down the room practicing exercises. More than an hour passed like a flash. He even played some of the Beethoven concerto at the end, before finishing as he always did with one of the Bach solo sonatas. While he was at this, he became aware that the priest was standing at the door watching him. He finished the piece, then laid the violin down carefully on the bed.

The priest said, "It's heavenly music, indeed. Have you ever played the Bach Double Concerto?"

"Often, with Papa. He and Mama were going to play it together on the evening of the day they were—they were—"

Suddenly, he found he couldn't say it. A cold, hard hand seemed to have gripped his chest, preventing the words from coming out.

"Would it be a good or a bad thing to play it with me?"

"A good thing, I think," Peter said after a long pause. "It's the music I love best in the world. I've played with a lot of people, not just with Papa. When any violinist came to the house, when I was only twelve or so, I used to ask them to play with me, eminent musicians of all kinds. They always agreed, though I'm sure they suffered agonies."

"I won't suffer. You probably will. Just wait while I get my violin and the music. Or do you know it from memory?"

"Not quite."

While the priest went to his room for his violin, Peter picked up his own again and found that his hands were sweating with excitement. The idea that had come to him before, that he might never again play music, seemed now to be buzzing around in his head like a trapped bee. But beside it, as clear as a summer morning, was the truth: that as long as he lived, music would be his first business. By the time the priest came back he was cool again and able to begin as if nothing had happened.

"Do you think we'd better use mutes?" Peter asked doubtfully.

"No. There's no one near enough to hear. It would spoil the music completely."

The priest was a much better musician than his words would have suggested. In fact, it was like playing with the best students in the conservatory, as Peter had often done when he could find one who was not too busy or too contemptuous of a junior student.

By the time they reached the middle of the slow movement, with its lovely swinging rhythm, the doorway was crowded with the rest of the household except for Mrs. Nagy. Peter wondered if she had indeed gone outside with the wolves, but when they finished and went downstairs they found that she was still sitting by the fire. Though she was not able to achieve a smile, she said quietly enough, "You play well together."

"Thank you. I was afraid you wouldn't like it—the sound, I mean."

"It sounds better in the country."

There could be no answer to that. For the rest of the evening she kept her good humor, and even helped a little in the kitchen when Agnes and Aunt Eva went to prepare supper. Pali watched Agnes milk the cow again, and had another try himself. There were eggs from the hens that rambled around the yard outside. Bread was a problem, Agnes said. She had waited for the bakery to be empty before asking for some extra.

"Though I don't believe anyone would talk about it if they saw me getting it," she said, "there's no harm in being careful. The Germans come around sometimes to check on how much bread is made, so as to find out if anyone is being hidden."

"I thought there were no Germans in the village," Aunt Eva said, alarmed.

"Not in the village. They're a few miles away. But they come now and then and one never knows when it will be. I've heard it said that the war is going against them— whether that will make them better or worse I don't know."

After supper the priest went out to visit a sick man and they all sat cozily by the fire, as if they were at home. There had been no word from the driver, though Agnes had seen him in the village with the mechanic.

"Of course he didn't show that he knew me," she said.

"He just gave me a glance as if he were curious and then turned away."

"Do you know him?" Aunt Eva asked.

"No, but I know his kind. He's safe enough."

"I wish we could stay here forever." That was Pali, of course.

Agnes said comfortably, "You'll come back when the war is over."

"When will that be? Once there was a hundred years' war, our teacher said."

"That was long ago. It's never like that nowadays."

"Sleeping in a real bed—that's a great thing."

"Many nights more, I hope," Agnes said. "You must wonder why I didn't welcome you when you came first."

"I can understand it," Aunt Eva said.

"Can you? He's so generous, he would take in anyone without thinking, if they came to the door. Some of them could be spies or thieves—he doesn't care. He says they're all sent by God. I say some of them come from the devil."

"Have you had some like that?"

"Oh, yes. One man went off with all the knives and forks. Said he was fleeing from the Germans. I think he was fleeing from the police. The priest said we're privileged to give charity." She snorted. "I'd give them charity, some of them. There are always people to take advantage of any situation. When I saw your driver at the door, I said, 'Here comes another sponger.' When you came in, I knew you were all right."

"Béla is reliable," Aunt Eva said. "So we have been told. I wish he would come back and tell us what's happening."

"I'd be glad if he didn't," Pali said. "Then we could stay here forever."

It was at that moment that they heard a soft double tap at the window. Agnes said, "There he is now. I told him to tap like that when he came back, so as not to give us all a fright. I'll go and let him in."

§ 14 §

Béla almost ran into the room, as if he would have liked to push past Agnes and get there before her. He held back, however, then stood by the door to gaze at the group sitting by the fire. No one spoke. After a moment he asked softly, "Where is the priest?"

"He went out," Agnes said. "An old man wanted to see him. He's been lying in bed for a long time; he gets anxious."

"You have bad news," Aunt Eva said softly. "Something has happened."

"That music," Béla said. "Someone heard it."

"Who?"

"The only person in the village who shouldn't have. She went to the Germans."

"We were told there are no Germans here."

"They're on an inspection. They come now and then. Usually they only stay a few hours. Why did you do it?"

"The priest thought it would be all right," Peter said. "He said there was no one to hear. We played the Bach Double together. He's a great musician."

"That's as may be. What do we do now?"

No one answered. Then Aunt Eva said, "How is the van?"

"Ready to roll. I didn't want to go in the middle of the night."

"Must we?"

"I don't know," Béla said restlessly. "They could come at any time."

A sound at the door made them all jump but it was only the priest returning. He came into the room, looked around sharply, and spoke directly to Béla. "Is everything all right?"

"I'm not sure. Old Sandor down at the mill came running into the garage to say that Anna—that's his wife, you know—was telling him that Veronika was out in the woods and heard the music and was on her way to tell the Germans that there must be Jews or angels, the music was so good."

"Veronika is a half-wit, God bless her," the priest said. "She hardly knows what day of the week it is."

"All the more reason for them to believe her, old Sandor says. She's not as silly as she pretends."

"What was she doing in the woods?"

"She told them she was gathering mushrooms."

"Mushrooms in March! That should prove she's talking nonsense. Surely they wouldn't believe her."

"You never know, with the Germans. They might say there were probably no mushrooms but there probably was music."

"I'd better go down. Where are they?"

"In Mark's tavern, of course. They're singing."

"What are they singing?"

"The usual:

'Wenn die Soldaten dürch die Stadt marschieren,
Öffnen die Mädchen Fenster und Türen—
Ei warum? Ei darum—' "

"That's enough—no need to sing it all. How many are there?"

"Six and an officer. The officer is not singing, only the men."

"What do you think I should do?"

"You could drop in at the tavern but they might wonder why, since you never go there in the ordinary way. Or you could get these people to hide in the forest with all their things, and wait here by yourself for the Germans to come. You'd have to have a good story to tell them."

"That would be the safest, I suppose. I have a record of the Bach Double that I could play for them, and say that's what Veronika must have heard."

Aunt Eva stood up at once and said, "We can't put you in danger. We'll move out into the woods." She turned to the others and said briskly, "Come along everyone."

They couldn't bear to look at each other. Heads down, everyone started up the stairs, watched helplessly by the priest and Agnes. At the top, Aunt Eva said, "Everyone put on your coat and take the bundle you started out with; and don't forget the violins."

"Of course we won't," Peter said angrily.

"I know. I'm only pulling your leg. Let's always laugh, whatever is happening."

Peter found himself laughing at the idea that there was something to laugh at, and he certainly felt better as he and David went into their room.

"How can she do it?" David asked as they began to

133

push their things into the bags and lay the violins back into their cases. "I wish I could have her philosophy."

"She told me once that she never looks back. She just tries to see what she has learned and go on from there. I think there's more to it than that. My father said she had a hard life when she was young. Her mother always told her she was good for nothing but housework, so she said that at least she would be good at that. I think she never had a chance to try anything else. Do what's next to be done, she always says. It's about all we can do now, anyway."

There was so little to carry, they were down again within a few minutes.

Then Béla said helplessly, "Perhaps I should go down for the van and we should head off up the mountain now, at once."

"They might wonder why you were going so late at night," the priest said. "Above all things we don't want them to search the van. Has anyone looked inside it?"

"No. There was no reason to. But you're right—even now, they might wonder why I'm not back in the tavern." Mrs. Nagy was standing at the foot of the stairs with her roll, the last to arrive. "Here, let me help you with that."

She almost struggled with him to hold it but he took it from her firmly and marched out of the house, carrying it on his shoulder. In single file they followed him up the path through the forest. The track was rough and there was very little light because the moon was not yet high enough to show above the dark trees. Stumbling over roots, sometimes almost falling, somehow they managed to go forward in the darkness until they came out at last in the nearest clearing, the one where they had rested on their walk that first day.

"Need we go any higher?" Aunt Eva asked. "If the soldiers come this far, we could run into the woods and hide among the trees."

"I suppose so." Béla dropped the roll on the ground, close to the edge of the grass. "Here, you can rest your backs against the trees. We should have brought a few blankets but I was afraid there was no time. Unless you hear them coming up the path, keep as still as mice. Agnes will help to send them in the wrong direction if they get too nosy. I'd better be off back to the village, before anyone wonders where I am. The priest will come for you when the coast is clear. Don't move until you see him."

They heard him moving softly down the hill, his boots making scarcely any sound on the thick carpet of pine needles. The moon came out from behind the trees suddenly and looked at them, lighting up the clearing like day. They began to settle down in the shadows under the thickest branches.

"It's so cold," Pali said miserably. " 'As still as mice,' he said. I wish we hadn't had to stop at all. I was used to the beastly old van. I don't like this forest. I wish we were back in Hungary, no matter what they were going to do to us."

"Quiet," Aunt Eva said in a strong whisper. "You can't just think of yourself."

"I want to go home," Pali said obstinately. "I don't want to be out on the side of a mountain in the cold. I want to go straight back to Budapest, to our own apartment, and live there again as we always did. I want to stay in our cottage and swim in Lake Balaton in the summer, and ride David's horse, and walk in the mountains—our own mountains—"

Suddenly he was wailing softly, saying over and over, "Mama, Mama. Papa, Papa," almost as if he thought they might come to him.

"Stop it, Pali," Peter said frantically, but Aunt Eva put her hand on his arm and squeezed it gently as she said to Pali, "We all want to go back but we can't. The time for all that is gone, for all of us." She pulled off her fur coat. "Here, sit close to me and wrap this around you. David, you come on his other side, and Suzy. You see, we'll be like a litter of pups, not like mice."

Suddenly, Mrs. Nagy began to scrabble with her bundle, with little grunts at the effort of pulling at the knots that tied it. She seemed to have a lot of trouble with it, even after she had got it unrolled.

"Help me with this," she said to Peter. "It's exactly what we need—my rugs. They're made of wool. We can sit on them and wrap them around us."

"But they'll be ruined. The ground is damp," Aunt Eva said.

"That's why we need them. They're only wool, after all. The people who made them can make more. It's just as well that I brought them along. We can use some of them as shawls."

No one spoke, afraid of making the wrong answer, until Pali said in an ugly tone, "What about the bears and the wolves? Won't they trample on your precious rugs?"

"There aren't many bears and wolves around here," Mrs. Nagy said. "That's only a story. You don't believe it, either. Here, get this rug under you."

136

"I don't have to do what you say."

"Pali! Do what you're told!" This time Aunt Eva sounded quite angry and Pali didn't dare to argue. Reluctantly, he allowed Mrs. Nagy to spread the rug close against the tree so that he could sit on it, and he watched while she took out three more for the others until they had a patchwork carpet on which they all squatted. Then, with the fur coat around him and lying close against Aunt Eva on one side and David and Suzy on the other, he became perfectly quiet, almost as if he were asleep.

Peter knew he was not asleep but at least he was no longer complaining. The things he had said had managed to make their plight seem much more desperate. Aunt Eva had said he would grow out of his habit of pointing out exactly what was wrong with every situation, but there was not much sign of improvement yet.

Peter was astonished, as they all were, at the change that had come over Mrs. Nagy but he didn't want to think of it. To be warm was the most important thing in the world at this moment. The soft feel of the wool rug that she had placed around his shoulders was the most delightful sensation in the world. It was so fine that it could hardly have been made for the floor. She must have had six of them in that roll of hers. Such fine rugs were immensely valuable. No wonder she was so careful of them.

He peered through the gloom toward the priest's house but there was very little to see, except for the dull glow of a candle from one window. Candles were such weak little things, and yet they were as old as the world and so important. He began to feel drowsy as the warmth spread through them from one to another. Like a litter of pups, Aunt Eva had said.

It seemed a long time before they heard the sound of a heavy truck coming up from the village. The air on the ground was perfectly still but the wind in the top branches of the pines was making its usual faraway, moaning song. Whatever was coming was having to move slowly because of the steep climb. Perhaps it was only a late driver on his way home. No one moved. It occurred to Peter now that if they had to escape into the forest, they would have to carry all their things with them. Chinks of moonlight showed among the branches of the tall trees. This would be their light.

The engine stopped on the road below and they could hear sharp voices, like the distant barking of dogs. Even through the still air it was impossible to hear what was being said, but the tones carried a threatening message. Dogs—Peter hadn't thought of them until now. If they had some with them, there would be no escape. Dogs couldn't be fooled. There was no hiding from them. But dogs would have begun to bark at once, if they were there, even well-trained German ones.

There was silence now. Still the little candle burned. Perhaps they were searching the house. Agnes would be showing them around with the lamp. She would have put away all signs of their occupation long ago, the used sheets and blankets that they had taken out to put on the beds. She would make the men some coffee or perhaps offer them some of her plum brandy.

All at once, like a whisper of rustling air, they heard the distant sound of music, weak, tinny, muffled at this distance, the unmistakable sound of a very old phonograph. It was playing the Bach Double Concerto. Peter almost laughed aloud. It was nothing like the music they had played earlier in the evening, when the two lovely instruments had blended so well together to make one voice. This was like two grasshoppers, he thought. Then, quite suddenly, the sound became strong and clear, carrying all the way up the mountainside to the silent listeners.

"It's the priest, playing along with the record," Peter whispered. "He's playing the first violin part this time."

"Quiet. Listen," Aunt Eva said.

The music went on for a few minutes, stopped and started again, obviously after the record had been changed. After that there was a pause: they heard the violin being tuned and a moment later the E-major solo sonata sang out into the night. At the end of the first movement there was a long pause, and then they heard the opening bars of the Chaconne. It went right through to the end, the intricate notes pouring out like the song of a crazy nightingale.

At last there was silence. Even with the rugs around them, everyone was beginning to feel the intense mountain cold, which is like no other sensation in the world. A small, uneasy ground wind had come up, and it found its way through to them by every nook and cranny. Still they waited, until at last they heard the loud voices again and the motor starting up. Very quietly now, the truck slid off down the mountain road. Within a few moments there was total silence.

They didn't have to wait long. There came the priest, almost running up the hill, his long, thin body leaning over as if he might fall, in his hurry to get to them. He called out as he came, "They've gone. Don't be afraid. You can come down now."

His long cassock sent the pine needles swirling as he helped them up, chattering all the time.

"Thank God the moon is shining. Carefully, please. Don't hurry. Agnes will have a big fire. Let me help you to roll up the rugs. I didn't know you had them—they're a blessing. Such a cold night to be out. The children first. Come along now, quickly. Agnes has hot milk and cakes. Run! Run!"

But it was not possible to run. At first it seemed that their legs had cramped up and were immovable, but gradually they limbered up as they hurried down toward the house, carrying their bundles. Though he was still angry with Pali, Peter took his bundle from him, saying, "You run ahead and tell Agnes we're coming."

With the two bundles banging against his legs, he was still laboring on when the priest and Aunt Eva and Mrs. Nagy caught up with him. The priest was carrying the precious rugs over his shoulder and helping Mrs. Nagy along. Sure enough, she had gone back to her whimpering but now Peter felt that she was entitled to, at least for a while.

The open doorway, with Agnes standing holding a candle high, was the most beautiful sight in the world.

§ 15 §

The fire on the hearth was so huge that Aunt Eva exclaimed, "Agnes! Are you planning to burn down the whole forest?"

"Come near, but not too near," Agnes said. "You must get warm gradually. That's always better. First you must drink something hot, then you can get as close as a cat to the heat."

"You seem to have experience."

"Yes. I've been out on the mountainside too, in my day, but that's all over now. I'll never forget the cold. Now give me those carpets and I'll hang them near the fire in the kitchen. It's the mercy of God that you had them. My goodness, they're beautiful! I hope they haven't suffered."

Peter was almost sorry for Mrs. Nagy as she looked over her precious rugs; she twisted her face so anxiously and stroked them as if they were alive. But then she gave them to Agnes and went to sit quietly at the table, where the children were already drinking hot milk. When the priest poured her some coffee she sat looking down into the cup as if to avoid everyone's eyes, until Aunt Eva said, "We would be a lot colder if Mrs. Nagy hadn't sacrificed her rugs for us to sit on. We all know what that meant to her."

"These times are full of small heroes," the priest said gently.

Mrs. Nagy looked pleased and embarrassed as she muttered, "They're only wool, only wool."

"Did you hear the music?" Agnes asked eagerly, coming back from the kitchen. "Such a concert! I never saw anything like it. The soldiers pushed past me as if they were going to arrest us all, poking into the rooms, peering under the beds, until Father came out of his room looking innocent and asked them if they needed something. The officer did a bit of barking at first but when he heard the story about the phonograph he said, 'So that's the explanation.' And Father said Veronika is not quite all there at the best of times, and probably the sight of the Germans in the village put ideas into her head. And then the officer asked to hear the record. He said he misses real music, he's sick and tired of hearing only marching songs. And he made the men sit down and listen. He said they could do with a bit of education."

The priest took up the story then.

"I was mighty glad to be able to oblige him. The phonograph doesn't always work. After a while the officer said, 'I wouldn't call that exactly angelic music.' He sounded a bit suspicious and I got a bad fright, but then I told him that I could never afford a good phonograph but that I often play my violin with the record as an accompaniment. I hope God will forgive me for all the lies I told. A thought came to me while I was talking to the officer, that at first I used to feel pity for the prisoners. Now I often feel pity for the guards."

"I don't waste sympathy on them," Agnes said with a snort. "They know very well what they're doing."

"Perhaps we'll find out someday. So he asked me to play, and I did. I was in practice from our concert this afternoon."

"We heard it, up in the forest," Aunt Eva said. "Then you played other pieces."

"Yes. He asked me if I could play anything else and I went through some more Bach until he said it was time to get back to the barracks. He thanked me for the concert and apologized for having disturbed me, and off they went."

"Why can't we stay here until the war is over?" Pali asked suddenly. "Now that they've come once, surely they won't come back."

"I wish I could be sure of that," the priest said, "but it's too dangerous. They might even pay us a visit tomorrow, to make sure they didn't let me off too easily. You'll be far safer in the Italian mountains. When all this is over you'll come to visit me, if I'm still here."

"Of course," Aunt Eva said hurriedly, sending a warning look to Pali about his manners.

"And you'll have the cow?" he persisted.

"We always have a cow," Agnes said.

Pali seemed satisfied with that. By this time everyone was almost falling asleep, from the heat of the fire and from the good feeling of safety. No one wanted to move, even when the priest said they should go to bed since they would have to make an early start in the morning.

"Béla is planning to come while it's still dark, so that you can get into the van without being seen," he said.

"He just hopes no one will notice that he has stopped here instead of keeping straight on up the mountain."

"How many more days?" Suzy's voice was shaking slightly as she asked the question.

"Two," Aunt Eva said firmly.

"Are you so sure?"

"Yes. I said we'll be there by the next Sabbath. This is Thursday, so it can only be two more days."

"I remember that you said that, but I've forgotten which day of the week it is," Peter said.

"Well, I can't forget, because of my prayers."

"Now you'll have mine as well," the priest said. "Bed, everyone."

They lay down in their clothes, since only Mrs. Nagy had untied her bundle. The wind had risen and was singing and wailing around the windows like someone asking to be let in. It was impossible to sleep. The minutes dragged on slowly. It seemed a lifetime since they had left the apartment in Budapest and hurried through the dark streets to where the van was parked. Peter began to think of his parents, where they were now, whether they had a bed to sleep in or were somewhere on one of those terrible trains, but then he had to put his fists in his eyes and roll himself tight in the blankets so as not to disturb David. There was no point in crying. Perhaps he would never cry again.

Before Béla arrived with the van they heard Agnes coming into the house. Downstairs, she had coffee and bread ready and was busy folding Mrs. Nagy's rugs, which had dried perfectly near the fire.

"They're beautiful," she said. "I hope you'll have them in a house of your own again, some day."

"Yes, they're beautiful," Mrs. Nagy said. "I'd like to give you one, after all you've done for us."

Agnes burst out laughing. "If you saw my house you wouldn't make that offer," she said. "I'm very grateful, but if one of my neighbors came in and saw a rug like that on the floor, they'd think I'd gone out of my mind. They'd certainly wonder where I got it. I hope I'm not insulting you."

"No, not at all."

Indeed, Mrs. Nagy did not look at all displeased and she tied up her bundle carefully again with a satisfied expression.

They hadn't quite finished eating when they heard the van arrive. The windows were still black except for the beam from the headlights. Peter wondered if he would ever get used to curtained windows, after experiencing the clear beauty of the surrounding night. It would depend on where one lived. He guessed that it was poverty that kept these windows free, and that there might be times when mountain people would prefer not to be gazed at by bears and wolves.

Béla had parked the van so that the secret door was exactly at the garden gate. He opened the back door for Peter to climb in and over the furniture, as he had done on the first day. Holding the flashlight, Peter looked around the tiny room. It was dismal and frightening. A sudden vision came to him of the door bursting open while they were inside, and the sharp voices barking orders to them to come out. They would be like mice in a nest—he couldn't get mice out of his head. No wonder Pali was always drawing them.

He peered through the peephole and saw the little group

standing there, with Béla, the priest, and Agnes who was holding a lantern. Pali's bear dangled from his arm and Suzy held her doll tucked under hers. They were all clutching their bundles. Peter opened the door quickly and the cramped room seemed to resume its life as they climbed in. Agnes had a bag with bread and a cake, which she had packed earlier. She handed this to Aunt Eva who hugged her hard for a moment.

"You'll come back," the priest said. "I'll be waiting for you. God bless you all. You're in good hands. I'll pray for you."

"In, quickly," Béla said in a sharp whisper. "And remember, no lights."

There was barely time for everyone to say good-bye before they were shut inside. At once they heard Béla hurrying around to the cab and climbing in. The engine started up and soon they were swinging around the mountain road again. Little by little the dawn came through the chinks, first in points like fireflies, then in broader streaks that gave enough light for them to see each other.

No one had the heart for games, but Aunt Eva insisted that they play chess and dominoes as before. Everyone except David and Mrs. Nagy grumbled, but Aunt Eva paid no attention. In a few minutes, she had Peter and Suzy playing a game of dominoes and she and Pali were playing cards.

"I thought you always said we shouldn't play cards," Pali said, "because it leads to fights."

"It takes two to make a fight," she said calmly, "and one must sometimes break one's own rules."

At noon, they ate bread and cheese and then some of Agnes's cake.

146

"After this," Pali said, "I'll never again complain about food."

"It was a good cake," Aunt Eva protested. "Everything Agnes cooks is good."

"I know it was good," Pali said, "but it wasn't as good as yours. A cake like that should be eaten in a warm kitchen, in good company."

"Listen to the child!" Mrs. Nagy said. "Where did you hear that?"

"Agnes said it herself, this morning. And anyway, everything tastes horrible while we're shut in here."

"No use pointing that out," Aunt Eva said sharply. "We're luckier than most."

Now that they knew what to expect, they barely paused to listen when the van stopped for fuel. But late in the afternoon they felt it slow down and heard shouts of *"Halten Sie, bitte!"* David put down the pawn he was holding and leaned across to take Suzy's hand. Gradually the van came to a stop and Béla climbed down and went to speak to the soldiers. After some more barking they heard him fumbling at the back door of the van. He lifted it noisily, and the light flooded in above the furniture. Aunt Eva closed her eyes and opened them again suddenly. Pali cowered down with his arms around his head. Suzy held David's hand tightly. Mrs. Nagy looked as if she had had a heart attack. Her eyes were fixed and staring and the chess piece in her hand seemed about to fall. Peter gazed at it, waiting for it to rattle down on to the floor, but she held on to it.

The whole van shook suddenly, as someone climbed up onto the back. Then they heard Béla say loudly, in German, "You see—officers' furniture. That's what I told you."

"I wouldn't mind owning some of that stuff," another voice said, "but if it belongs to an officer we'd better leave it alone. Where is it going?"

"Sondrio," Béla said. "I hear it's a rotten road."

"I've never been there. It's a long way, I think." And then came the welcome shout, *"Alles in Ordnung!"*

The door slammed shut and they could hear the lock being turned. A minute later Béla was back in the cab and they were moving again, this time very slowly. Aunt Eva put her finger on her lips to warn against any sound. Peter felt a cramp in one leg but he was afraid to stretch it yet. Sure enough, after no more than two minutes they were stopped again. Béla shouted out of the cab window, "I've been passed. The last man searched me."

"Open up. We have to search twice. New orders."

Béla jumped down. "Anything you like. You're the boss. How's the war going? I never hear any news."

"No news is good news. They say we're winning. We might be home for the summer."

"What do you want to see?"

The back door was opened again. Peter saw that tears were running down Mrs. Nagy's cheeks and she was breathing heavily. He wanted to lean over and take her hand, as David was doing for Suzy, but he was afraid she would not like it. Better to leave her alone and hope she wouldn't begin to shriek hysterically. He felt himself breathing faster. Courage was what he needed, if only he knew what courage was.

The officer was saying, "You'll have to take out all that stuff and let me see it."

148

"Why? I know it's not my business to ask but aren't you making a lot of work for yourself?"

"That's all right. I'm bored to death here anyway. I'll help you. We'll have it done in a few minutes. You know, in the army we always have to show enthusiasm. It's not quite enough to do what we're told, though they always say it is. A soldier's first duty is to obey—but if that's all he does he never gets promoted. Come on—we'll begin with the boxes."

Aunt Eva stretched out her arms gently, as if she were asking for something to be put into them, and her lips moved slightly as she prayed. Pali's head came up and Peter saw that he was staring at her with a wild look. Then came Béla's voice again, saying, "I'm bored, too, with all this fetching and carrying. You think it will be over soon?"

"The war? Of course. You can't beat the German army."

"In that case we might just as well enjoy ourselves. How about a game of cards?"

"It's forbidden to play cards on duty."

"Do you mean to stay in the army when the war is over?"

"Catch me! I'll look for a job in Milan or Paris and go into business after a while. It will be easy, you'll see."

"So why don't we have a game of cards, instead of rooting through all that junk?"

"Suits me, as you put it like that. Have you got a pack?"

"Yes, in the cab. Hold on there and I'll get it."

"It's starting to rain," the soldier said. "Everything will get wet."

"You're right," Béla said, sounding disappointed. "Heavy, too. Maybe we could sit in here at the back, behind the furniture. It's a bit dirty but we won't mind that."

want to shout out in terror. He always woke up in time to avoid this, then fell asleep again soon afterward.

When the van stopped, he was the first awake. It was after eight o'clock. A few points of yellow light filtered in through the cracks, as if they were in a village street. One by one the others woke up, stretching a little but perfectly quiet. All Peter could see was their shadowy forms. The engine was switched off and Béla got out. A moment later they heard him talking to someone. He sounded cheerful and relaxed but they couldn't hear what he was saying. Peter guessed that he was asking about a night's lodging and safe parking for the van. So it turned out. The van was moved again, then halted, and since Béla made no attempt to speak to them, Peter guessed that he was parked in a place where he thought this would not be safe. In any case, none of them would have wanted to open the door now. After last night's terrors, the only safe place seemed to be inside the van with both doors tightly shut.

It was a quiet village, but Peter listened with sharpened senses for every tiny sound. An occasional night bird shrieked and some cats started a fight but gave it up quite soon. After that, not even a dog barked during the night and there were no soldiers stamping about and shouting. There was the sound of a fast river, which meant that they were still in the mountains, and the air felt light and clear. When he slept at last, Peter no longer woke in panic, and he even found it hard to open his eyes in the morning when the van moved off again.

While they were eating some of Agnes's cake Pali said, "It's the Sabbath, and we're not free yet."

"The Sabbath is not over," Aunt Eva said. "Just wait. Just have patience."

152

Not long afterward they stopped suddenly, and they heard Béla shouting in German, "Out of the way, you idiot! Do you want me to run over you?"

A soft voice answered excitedly, and a moment later there was Béla actually banging at the secret door, saying loudly, "Come out, come out! We're there!"

Still, Peter put his eye to the peephole before opening the door. A tall, thin man in a sheepskin jacket was standing beside Béla, moving from heel to toe almost as if he were getting ready to run away. Peter opened the door and stepped down onto the road.

"It's a shepherd from your village. He's going to take you there. Come along, everyone."

"Are we going to walk?" Mrs. Nagy squawked indignantly as she climbed down after the others.

"It's not far," Béla said. "Only a mile or so, up there." He turned to the man again and was obviously telling him the names of the places they had passed through: Stuben, then Stelvio and Bormio. The shepherd seemed astonished that they had come so far, and he waved and pointed toward the mountainside.

It rose almost directly from the road. Melting snow sent channels running down its sides in little streams that glinted in the sunlight. On the other side the land dropped sheer down into a deep valley, with alternating rocks and green patches where sheep were grazing.

Béla spoke to the man again, then said, "He tells me there's another valley a little higher up. That's the one you're going to. Down there is Valle di Sotto; up above is Valle di Dentro, which means 'the inside valley.' You won't go quite as high as that—you'll be somewhere in between. No one goes there except the people who live there."

153

"Is he a cousin of Mrs. Rossi?" Aunt Eva asked.

"No, but he knows all the cousins. They sent him down to meet you. He says he's been waiting for two days. That would be while you were at the priest's house."

"Has he been outside all this time?" Aunt Eva asked, horrified.

Béla asked the man this question and he laughed, pointing to the sheep as he answered. He had been in a hut, Béla said, where he often slept at lambing time.

"What language is that? It sounds like Italian but it's not really the same. I wish I knew it, so that I could thank him."

"It's Romansh," Béla said. "I know a little from driving through here often. You'll learn quickly. And most people here also speak Italian, though this man doesn't."

"Then it will be easy. I know Italian quite well. The children, too. They learned it at school, along with German and French. I often spoke it with Mrs. Rossi."

"Good. He says they had some Gypsies a while ago. You know they were being collected by the Germans, too. But they only spoke their own language and no one was able to understand them. They moved on after a while so you'll be the only visitors. You'll be in good hands."

"Then you're not coming with us," Aunt Eva said.

"No. It would be dangerous for you and for me, too. And I must take this furniture to Sondrio. The officer will be expecting it. Now, have you got all your things safely?"

"Yes, everything. How can we ever thank you?"

"We'll talk about that when the war is over, when I see you again. I'll find you, never fear."

"You are hopeful about the future?"

"Hopeful? I don't know. I trust in God and live from one day to the next. What else can one do?"

"You'll pass this way again?"

"Of course. I'll have to play a game of cards with that soldier."

Even Mrs. Nagy joined in as they all thanked him and wished him a safe journey. He shook hands with them one by one, finishing with Pali, saying, "I have a boy your age at home. I've thought of him a lot this week."

Then he was off, climbing up into the cab of his van and driving slowly down the steep road while they stood in a group and watched him. When he had gone out of sight around a bend, their guide waved toward the mountainside where a narrow path, perhaps made by goats or mules, wriggled upward. Shouldering their bundles, they started to follow him, Mrs. Nagy whimpering miserably at the very idea of what was before her. The shepherd turned back and said a few words to her, taking her roll firmly from her as he did so. She began to protest but then thought better of it, and followed close behind him as he started up the track. The others went in single file after her.

Zigzagging around the mountainside, it was almost an hour before the shepherd stopped and waited for them. There was no question of resting, since he was always a hundred yards ahead and moving fast. The track ran with water and soon their shoes were soaked through. The air was colder and thinner up here, making it hard to breathe, but each turn in the path was a small relief because the slope was a little less steep for a minute or two afterward. At last they came up with the shepherd and stood beside him.

They were looking down into a long, green valley, which climbed gently on all sides toward the high mountains. A river flowed at one side of it and streams ran from the river toward the various houses that were scattered here and there all over the valley. Some small houses clung to the side of the mountain with green patches in front where sheep and cattle grazed. Their guide pointed out places, giving their names, though he knew that no one could understand him. The river seemed to be called the Ada. Like her doll, Suzy said.

Then the shepherd was climbing downward, followed cautiously by Mrs. Nagy and Aunt Eva, then by the rest of them. Going down was much harder, as there was a sensation of sliding and falling on the narrow path and each step had to be considered carefully. The shepherd seemed to find it quite easy. As they moved along, every now and then the valley floor disappeared from view when they turned the shoulder of the mountain.

At last the rocks gave way to grass and they were crossing a broad meadow. Now for the first time they saw people moving about near the houses, and then a steady stream of men, women, and children began to run toward them as they toiled wearily along. David and Suzy trudged behind Aunt Eva, who kept telling Mrs. Nagy that there were only a few more steps to go. From his position at the end of the procession, Peter watched Pali anxiously. His head was down and he was gazing at his feet as if he would never be able to look up again. Peter felt a spurt of rage dart through him, at the thought that such a small boy should have had to endure what Pali had. He called out, "Pali! Look! Everyone is coming! Leave your things and go down to them. I'll carry everything for you."

But it was no use. At least he was not crying. He was probably too tired even for that, Peter thought, though he did lift his head as he almost staggered under his load. Then they were surrounded by the crowd, all talking and laughing and asking questions. Looking at Aunt Eva, one would think she had known them all her life. Within five minutes she had found out which ones were Mrs. Rossi's cousins, and she even knew them apart—Carlo who was married to Franca, and Serafino who was married to Angelina, Donata and Tonino who were their closest neighbors. She named everyone in her own party and asked after Peppino and Nello and their wives and children. She was told that they would get messages in no time and would be in the valley before the evening was out.

The bundles were grabbed by the men, and for the first time they were able to walk free.

In a cheerful procession they moved along toward the nearest house, which stood a little apart from the others. Not all of the neighbors could fit inside but they stayed around the door watching, while those who were able to get in helped Mrs. Nagy first to a chair by the fire in the parlor. Donata, whose house it was, knelt down and took off Mrs. Nagy's shoes for her and rubbed her feet, while Aunt Eva stood by for a moment with an amused smile before sitting down at the table. Peter dropped into the chair beside her.

"That one will never be different," she said, nodding in the general direction of Mrs. Nagy. "She had a short try at improving herself but she wasn't able to keep it up. You'll see how things will go."

Sure enough, after everyone had been given coffee and cake and had had a short rest, they went outside to look at the farm buildings and animals. But Mrs. Nagy stayed firmly indoors and by the time they got back from their inspection she had installed herself in one of the bedrooms. She was coming down the stairs as they came into the house.

"There's only room for one of us here," she said to Aunt Eva, "so I thought I had better move in. You can go to the other houses. I really couldn't have walked another step. And that child who draws the mice will be glad to get away from me, you may be sure."

"No, no," Aunt Eva said seriously. "We have all been glad to have you with us. But do stay here if you like. We won't be far away, I think."

So the rest of the party had to set out again, though this time it was much easier, since they were able to see where they were going and they knew their hosts. Aunt Eva and Pali and Suzy were to go to Carlo and Franca's house, David and Peter to Serafino and Angelina. This was no hardship as the houses were side by side. Both of the families had children of their own, girls and boys of all ages, though it was hard to work out which ones belonged to each house.

Already the parents were trying to make contact with the strangers in a mixture of Italian and Romansh. Though they didn't pronounce Italian as the teacher did in Budapest, it was not difficult to understand them. Peter heard Pali ask cautiously, *"Dov'è la vacca?"*

A boy of his own age answered immediately, *"Qui, qui!"*

He darted before him into the cow shed. Peter followed them and saw Pali gazing in wonder and delight at a huge, pale cow with big brown eyes, while she gazed back at him.

"Isn't she beautiful?" he whispered. "Do you think they'll let me milk her?"

"I'm sure they will, when they know you can do it. And we'll all have to work, to earn our living. I think they'll be pleased."

"I might start drawing cows now, instead of mice. These cows don't look frightened at all."

The violins caused great interest, and Serafino said they would have many a concert in the future.

"What about the sound? Won't the neighbors mind?" Aunt Eva asked.

"Not at all. I play the georgina myself," Serafino said, and he made gestures of squeezing an accordian in and out to show what a georgina was.

At their house, as soon as they had seen where they were to sleep, Aunt Eva asked Franca if she could make a cake. "But only if you have eggs and flour," she said. "I don't want to be a nuisance. This is our Sabbath and if it's at all possible we should have a celebration of some kind for it."

"Certainly," Franca said. "We have everything you need—sugar, too. I got some last week and I was keeping it for when the children would arrive. I know it's your big day in the week, and now we can all celebrate it together."

They disappeared into the kitchen, and soon the familiar delicious smells began to spread through the house.

As the evening went on, the other cousins and their families began to arrive at Serafino and Angelina's house. It had the bigger parlor of the two, with a long central table and chairs, and covered benches at either side of the hearth. There was still space for an upright piano at one end, and David went at once to have a look at it. It was

159

an old German piano of a very good make. He lifted the lid cautiously and saw that it had been well looked after. With luck it might not be too badly out of tune. Suzy was able to play a little, and since there was no hope of a cello for her, perhaps he would be able to help her with the piano instead.

The room was quickly filled to overflowing. News had to be given of the Rossis, then there was a little talk about the war, which was so remote from this valley that it might have been taking place in another world. The men shook their heads at the terrible things that were being done to innocent people. The cake was brought in from next door and there was enough for everyone, and a glass of very precious sweet wine to go with it.

Mrs. Nagy and her hosts arrived in time for this. She was looking a little less acid than when they had seen her last, and she even smiled politely when Serafino brought out his georgina and began to play a mountain love song. She soon said she was tired, however, and left to go to bed. As she passed by David, who was sitting with Suzy on one of the benches near the fire, she said, "We can have a game of chess tomorrow."

"Of course," David said. "I'll be glad to, after I've practiced the piano."

"Perhaps they won't allow it," she said, leaning down and whispering hoarsely. "Some people are very careful of their possessions."

"I think they won't mind," David said. "They like music."

"You call that music?" She gave a strange little titter. "That's a peasant noise, nothing else. Well, you can have a try, I suppose."

And she sailed out. As she had been speaking in Hungarian, the people who were sitting near had not understood what she said. But one man said after a moment, "She's upset at having to leave her home, I think. She looks much more miserable than the rest of you."

"That will improve as time goes on," another said, nodding wisely. "She'll settle down when she finds that she's with friends."

There was a short pause, as if no one liked to contradict this, then Serafino said, "I saw two violins. Who plays them?"

"My little brother plays one," Peter said. "I play the other. The one I play belonged to my father."

"Your father?"

"Yes." Peter glanced anxiously at Pali who had his head down again and was looking angrily at the floor. "My father was taken away by the Germans. He was a well-known violinist in Hungary, *molto conosciuto*, big." He made a wide gesture with his hands. His Italian was not sufficient to say any more, but Serafino was nodding his head to show that he understood. Peter went on, "Our friend David plays the piano."

"Then we'll have concerts! This is wonderful—you will all play for us, that is, if you don't mind."

He was suddenly uneasy, glancing at Aunt Eva, but she said, "Yes, they will play. They love to play. Go and get your violin. You can bring along Pali's, too."

"You mean, now?"

"Yes," Aunt Eva said in Hungarian. "Everyone is so good to us, and they would be so pleased. You can play the Beethoven sonata that you played with David last month."

161

"The Spring sonata? We know it by heart. But we'll play badly. We're too tired."

"Nonsense. It's not a public concert. It will do you good."

There was a great air of excitement as a space was made around the piano and Peter went to fetch his violin. It was true that the thought of playing had made him feel suddenly better, as if a load that he had been carrying for weeks had been taken away from him. When he came back he found that David was softly trying out the piano, playing chords and gently running his fingers up and down the keyboard to see if it was in tune. Of course it was not, but now it didn't seem to matter. The expectant, smiling faces all around the room, and the extra ones in the doorway, made such a thought seem trivial. Now the important thing was to give pleasure, however simple, to these good people, and Peter found that he had never before played in such a relaxed, happy way. The strangeness of this happiness didn't have to be explained. It simply seemed to live alongside the tearing pain that filled his whole body at the loss of his parents, as if the two so different sensations were meant to keep each other company.

When they had finished Angelina said, "And now the smaller boy—you will play for us, won't you? Just a little, please, Pali."

Peter watched breathlessly as Pali paused for a long moment. He seemed to go through a big struggle before he said, speaking directly to her, "I'll play one piece for you, that I know by heart."

And he began to play Smetana's beautiful piece called "From the Homeland." His bow wobbled a little on the first long notes, where the splendid ninths follow each other before going into the melody. David, who was still sitting at the piano, came in with the accompaniment and Pali gave him a delighted look. After that he was steady as a rock, his face concentrated and the music seeming to flow out in a long bright stream, until the last gentle notes fell softly at the close. There was complete silence as he put his violin down, then Angelina said, "It's the music of the angels, indeed."

Aunt Eva had already told the story of the terrible night when the priest and Peter had played the Bach Double Concerto and had been overheard. Now while everyone thanked Peter and Pali for the concert, she had to tell the story to the whole company. While this was going on, Pali had time to get out his handkerchief and dry the tears that had fallen on his violin, and put it safely on top of the piano.

That was the first of many concerts. They always began with Serafino taking out the georgina and saying, "First my mountain music, then the music of heaven."

Mrs. Nagy never stayed for these concerts, and she never did settle down. Aunt Eva did her best but even she had to give up after a while. Everything upset Mrs. Nagy, the sound of the cowbells in the early morning as the cows made their way to the high pastures, a sudden late fall of snow, the shouts of the men as they came in from their day's logging, the occasional visits of the young men who were away at the war and were able to get home for a few days, the good news and the bad news. Donata was so patient that the whole valley said she was a saint. Only sometimes she would appear at Angelina's door and say, "David, can you come over and play a game of chess with her? She's driving everyone crazy with her complaints."

163

And David was very willing to go, but only in the afternoons, since by now the routine of morning practice was once more established. Aunt Eva made sure that nothing interfered with this.

"After all," she said, "whatever happens in the outside world, life must go on for the rest of us. Some day the war will be over and we'll have to carry on as usual."

"How can we carry on, after the things that have happened?" David said. "I have no home, no family now."

"You don't know that, for certain. We must live in hope. They may come back. And if they don't, you still have a family. You belong to us. You must learn to forget the bad things and remember the good ones."

"Is that possible?"

"I think so. At least, it's what I've done all my life," Aunt Eva said.

"Will Suzy be able to forget?"

"Yes, if you help her. We'll all have to help each other."

"And the music? Do you think we'll always have that?"

"Of course. The world will always need music."